5

Minute
Bedtime Classics

5
Minute
Bedtime Classics

FOR
YOUNG
READERS

First published in various editions from c. 1890–1923.

First Racehorse for Young Readers Edition 2019.

Racehorse for Young Readers books may be purchased in bulk at special discounts for sales promotion, corporate gifts, fund-raising, or educational purposes. Special editions can also be created to specifications. For details, contact the Special Sales Department, Racehorse for Young Readers, 307 West 36th Street, 11th Floor, New York, NY 10018 or info@skyhorsepublishing.com.

Racehorse for Young Readers™ is a pending trademark of Skyhorse Publishing, Inc.®, a Delaware corporation.

Visit our website at www.skyhorsepublishing.com.

10 9 8 7 6 5 4 3 2 1

Library of Congress Cataloging-in-Publication Data is available on file.

Cover design by Brian Peterson
Book design by Daniel Brount

Print ISBN: 978-1-63158-341-4
Ebook ISBN: 978-1-63158-343-8

Printed in China

Contents

Jack and the Beanstalk

ONCE upon a time there was a boy named Jack who was his mother's only child. They were very poor, so poor that one day his mother said, "Jack, we shall have to sell our cow. Take Bossy to the market and get as much money as you can for her." On the way Jack met a little old man who offered him some colored beans in exchange for the cow. Jack thought they were very pretty and traded Bossy for them. When his mother learned what he had done, she was very angry and threw the beans out the window.

The next morning when Jack awoke he saw something strange in his yard. It was a magic beanstalk which had grown from the beans high up into the sky. Jack climbed the beanstalk and there at the top he found a great castle. A lovely fairy stood at the gate. "Welcome, Jack," she said. "This is the castle of the wicked giant who killed your father. You must get back the riches he stole from you and your mother."

Jack thanked the fairy for her kindness and knocked at the castle gate. When the giant's wife saw how tired and hungry he was after his long journey, she brought him in to give him some food. Suddenly there was a loud noise and she cried, "Quick! The giant is coming! You must hide in the cupboard." Jack ran and hid and watched the giant as he ate his supper.

Then the giant called for his pet hen and when it was put on the table he roared, "Lay me an egg!" And the magic hen laid a golden egg. When Jack saw that the giant was asleep, he slipped from his hiding place and tucking the hen under his arm ran for home. After that he and his mother lived in comfort for the hen laid them a golden egg every day.

One day Jack climbed the beanstalk again and this time he brought home two money bags. A third time he went to get his father's golden harp. As he was leaving the castle, the giant heard him and rushed out after him and followed him down the beanstalk. Jack called to his mother to bring him an ax. As soon as he touched the ground, he seized the ax and chopped the beanstalk. It broke in two and the giant crashed to the ground. Then Jack and his mother lived happily ever after.

Chicken Little

ONE summer day Chicken Little felt a leaf fall on her tail. She ran to Henny Penny, crying, "Oh, Henny Penny, the sky is falling! I saw it with my eyes. I heard it with my ears. I felt it on my tail."

"Dear me!" said Henny Penny, "we must go and tell the king."

Soon they met Ducky Lucky. "The sky is falling!" cried Henny Penny.

"How do you know, Henny Penny?" "Chicken Little told me."

"How do you know, Chicken Little?" "I saw it with my eyes. I heard it with my ears. I felt it on my tail."

"Dear me!" said Ducky Lucky, "we must go and tell the king."

Soon they met Goosey Loosey. "The sky is falling!" cried Ducky Lucky.

"How do you know, Ducky Lucky?" "Henny Penny told me."

"How do you know, Henny Penny?" "Chicken Little told me."

"How do you know, Chicken Little?" "I saw it with my eyes. I heard it with my ears. I felt it on my tail."

"Dear me!" said Goosey Loosey, "we must go and tell the king."

Soon they met Turkey Lurkey. "The sky is falling!" cried Goosey Loosey.

"How do you know, Goosey Loosey?" "Ducky Lucky told me."

"How do you know, Ducky Lucky?" "Henny Penny told me."

"How do you know, Henny Penny?" "Chicken Little told me."

"How do you know, Chicken Little?" "I saw it with my eyes. I heard it with my ears. I felt it on my tail."

"Dear me!" cried Turkey Lurkey, "we must go and tell the king."

Soon they met Foxy Loxy. "The sky is falling!" cried Turkey Lurkey.

"How do you know, Turkey Lurkey?"
"Goosey Loosey told me."

"How do you know, Goosey Loosey?"
"Ducky Lucky told me."

"How do you know, Ducky Lucky?"
"Henny Penny told me."

"How do you know, Henny Penny?"
"Chicken Little told me."

"How do you know, Chicken Little?"
"I saw it with my eyes. I heard it with my ears. I felt it on my tail. We are going to tell the king."

"But, I am the king," said Foxy Loxy. "Come into my den and we shall decide what to do."

So Chicken Little, Henny Penny, Ducky Lucky, Goosey Loosey, and Turkey Lurkey all went into Foxy Loxy's den.

But they never came out again, foolish birds.

This is the House that Jack Built

This is the **HOUSE**
that Jack built.

This is the **MALT**
That lay in the House
that Jack built.

This is the **RAT**
That ate the Malt
That lay in the House
that Jack built.

This is the **CAT**
That teased the Rat
That ate the Malt
That lay in the House
that Jack built.

This is the **DOG**
That worried the Cat
That teased the Rat that
    ate the Malt
That lay in the House that
    Jack built.

This is the **COW** with the
    crumpled horn
That tossed the Dog
That worried the Cat
That teased the Rat that
    ate the Malt
That lay in the House
    that Jack built.

This is the **MAIDEN** all
  forlorn
That milked the Cow with
  the crumpled horn
That tossed the Dog
That worried the Cat
That teased the Rat that ate
  the Malt
That lay in the House that
  Jack built.

This is the **MAN** all tattered
  and torn
That kissed the Maiden all
  forlorn
That milked the Cow with
  the crumpled horn
That tossed the Dog
That worried the Cat
That teased the Rat that ate
  the Malt
That lay in the House that
  Jack built.

This is the **PRIEST** all
  shaven and shorn
That married the Man all tat-
  tered and torn
That kissed the Maiden all
  forlorn
That milked the Cow with
  the crumpled horn
That tossed the Dog
That worried the Cat
That teased the Rat that ate
  the Malt.
That lay in the House that
  Jack built.

The Sleeping Beauty

ONCE long ago, a baby girl was born to a king and queen. They invited all the good fairies to the christening party but they forgot the one bad fairy in the kingdom. When the christening day came, all the fairies flew in at the palace window and brought their gifts to the sleeping princess. The first gave her beauty; the second, grace; the third, a happy heart; and the fourth, a quick wit. Eleven good fairies made their magic wishes and the twelfth

stood beside the crib wondering what to give. Suddenly, the
bad fairy rushed forward. She was angry because she had not
been invited to the party. In a voice of thunder she cried,
"My gift to you shall be that on your eighteenth birthday you
will prick your finger with a spindle and die."

At that moment the last of the good fairies stepped forward and said, "Do not mourn, Oh, King and Queen. My gift
shall be that when your daughter pricks her finger she will

not die but will fall asleep for a hundred years until a prince shall awaken her with a kiss." Immediately the king ordered that all the spindles in the kingdom be burned so that the princess could not prick her finger on one.

Now, on her eighteenth birthday, the princess found her way to the highest turret of the castle where she had never been before. There she saw a little old woman spinning. By accident she pricked her finger on the spindle and at that same moment she fell to the floor in a deep slumber. Everyone in the castle fell asleep when the princess did.

As the years went by, many princes came to try to rescue the sleeping beauty, but a thorny hedge had sprung up around the castle and each gave up. But after a hundred years the spell was broken and the prince who was meant for her came. Then the hedge disappeared, the gates swung open, and the princess awoke when the prince kissed her. The whole house came suddenly to life; the king and queen and all their court crowded about the prince to thank him for rescuing them. But he asked only one reward, the hand of the princess in marriage. Gladly the king and queen granted his wish. And the magic day ended in feasting and merrymaking.

The Old Woman
and Her Pig

AN OLD woman was once driving her pig down the road toward home. When she came to a stile, she could not make the pig jump over it.

Then the old woman saw a dog. She asked the dog to bite the pig but the dog would not.

Then she met a stick. She asked the stick to beat the dog but the stick would not.

Then she came to a fire. She asked the fire to burn the stick but the fire would not.

Then she saw some water. She asked the water to quench the fire but the water would not.

Then she met a cow. She asked the cow to drink the water but the cow would not.

Then she met a butcher. She asked the butcher to drive the cow but the butcher would not.

Then she saw a rope. She asked the rope to tie the butcher but the rope would not.

Then she met a rat. She asked the rat to gnaw the rope. The rat answered, "Bring me a piece of cheese and I will."

So the old woman gave the rat a piece of cheese and then:

The rat began to gnaw the rope, the rope began to tie the butcher, the butcher began to drive the cow, the cow began to drink the water, the water began to quench the fire, the fire began to burn the stick, the stick began to beat the dog, the dog began to bite the pig, the pig went over the stile and so the old woman got home.

BUTCHER FIRE STICK DOG CHEESE ROPE WATER PIG RAT COW

The
Frog Prince

ONE day a beautiful princess sat crying by the edge of a deep pool in her garden. She had lost her golden ball in the pool. Just then a voice spoke to her and, looking up, she saw that it was a frog.

"Do not cry, Princess," said the frog. "I will get your ball for you if you will make me a promise."

"What is it?" asked the princess.

"It is this," said the frog. "You must let me eat from your little gold plate and sleep on your little white pillow."

The princess eagerly promised so the frog dived into the pool and brought her ball to her.

At dinner time there was a queer noise at the castle gate. The frog had come to eat from her little gold plate and to sleep on her little white pillow. The princess longed to send him away but she remembered her promise. At bedtime she let the frog lie on her little white pillow. Suddenly he disappeared and a handsome prince stood beside her. "Who are you?" cried the princess.

"A wicked witch turned me into a frog," the prince explained. "I could never take my own shape until a princess let me eat from her plate and sleep on her pillow. You have saved me."

Then the prince and princess were married and they lived happily ever after.

The Gingerbread Boy

A LITTLE old woman and a little old man lived in a little house. They were very lonely, because they had no children.

One day the little old woman said, "I will make me a little Gingerbread Boy, then I can pretend that he is my boy."

So she made a Gingerbread Boy. She gave him eyes, a nose, and a mouth made of sugar-frosting. The buttons on his jacket were black currants. When he was all ready, she put him in the oven to bake.

After awhile it became very hot in the oven. The Gingerbread Boy cried in a loud voice, "Let me out! Let me out!"

The little old woman came running, and opened up the oven door. The Gingerbread Boy jumped out and ran away calling—

"I'm a little Gingerbread Boy, I am, I am,
I can run away from you, I can, I can."

The little old woman picked up her skirts and ran after him, as fast as she could run, but—*she couldn't catch him.*

The little old man was hoeing in the garden. He ran after the Gingerbread Boy, but the Gingerbread Boy called back—

"I'm a little Gingerbread Boy, I am, I am,
I can run away from you, I can, l can.
I ran away from a little old woman,
And I can run from you, I can, I can."

The little old man dropped his hoe and ran after him, as fast as he could run, but—*he couldn't catch him.*

On and on ran the Gingerbread Boy till he came to a field where men were mowing hay. The Gingerbread Boy called out—

"I'm a little Gingerbread Boy, I am, I am,
I can run away from you, I can, I can.
I ran away from a little old woman, a little old man,
And I can run from you, I can, I can."

The men stopped mowing and ran after the Gingerbread Boy, lickity-cut, but—*they couldn't catch him.*

On and on ran the Gingerbread Boy till he came to a big barn full of threshers. He waved his arms and called—

"I'm a little Gingerbread Boy, I am, I am,
I can run away from you, I can, I can.
I ran away from a little old woman, a little old man,
A field full of mowers,
And I can run from you, I can, I can."

The men stopped threshing and ran after the Gingerbread Boy, but—*they couldn't catch him.*

On and on ran the Gingerbread Boy till he came to a pasture where an old red cow was eating clover. He called out—

"I'm a little Gingerbread Boy, I am, I am,
I can run away from you, I can, I can.
I ran away from a little old woman, a little old man,
A field full of mowers, a barn full of threshers,
And I can run from you, I can, I can."

The old cow stopped eating clover and ran after the Gingerbread Boy, as fast as she could run, but—*she couldn't catch him.*

On and on ran the Gingerbread Boy until by and by he met a big fat pig who was eating corn off the cob. The Gingerbread Boy waved his arms, and ran across the bridge, calling—

"I'm a little Gingerbread Boy, I am, I am, ·
I can run away from you, I can, I can.
I ran away from a little old woman,
A little old man,

A field full of mowers,
A barn full of threshers,
An old red cow,
And I can run away from you, I can, I can."

The pig stopped eating and said, "Oomph! Oomph!" and ran after the Gingerbread Boy, but—*he couldn't catch him.*

On and on ran the Gingerbread Boy far into a big, dark forest, where
he saw a sly old fox. The fox pretended he was taking a nap, but he had
one eye open. The Gingerbread Boy thought he was asleep so he came
close to the old fox, and called out—

"I'm a little Gingerbread Boy, I am, I am,
l can run away from you, I can, I can.

I ran away from a little old woman,
A little old man,
A field full of mowers,
A barn full of threshers,
An old red cow,
A big fat pig,
And I can run away from you, I can, I can."

All of a sudden the fox opened both eyes and his mouth, too, and he bit off one of the Gingerbread Boy's legs.

"Yum! Yum!" said the fox. "That Gingerbread Boy tastes good."

"Oh dear! Oh dear!" cried the Gingerbread Boy. "One leg is all gone. Now I can't run very well!"

Then the fox ate the other leg. And he said, "Yum! Yum! That Gingerbread Boy tastes very good!"

"My two legs are all gone," said the Gingerbread Boy. "Now I can't run at all!"

"Yum! Yum!" said the fox, and he ate the Gingerbread Boy's jacket with the currants on it.

"I'm half gone!" wailed the Gingerbread Boy.

The fox ate off one of the Gingerbread Boy's arms. He licked his chops, and said, "Yum! Yum! That Gingerbread Boy tastes very, very good."

"One arm all gone!" wailed the Gingerbread Boy.

Then the fox ate the other arm.

"My two arms are all gone!" wailed the Gingerbread Boy.

The fox opened his mouth wide and gulped down the rest of the Gingerbread Boy. "Now I'm all gone!" said a wee small voice from way inside the fox.

And that was the end of the Gingerbread Boy.

Hansel
and Gretel

ONCE upon a time a poor woodcutter lived with his wife and two children near a great forest. The boy was called Hansel and the girl, Gretel. They were often hungry, for they were poor and did not have enough to eat. One night the man said to his wife,

"We have little food left to eat in the house, and I do not know what to do."

"There would be more food for us if we got rid of the children," said the wife. "Tomorrow we will take them into the forest. We will make a fire and leave them to rest by it. We will go off to our work and they will never find the way home."

"Oh, but I cannot leave my children to the wild beasts of the woods," said the man.

"Then we will all starve," said the woman.

Now the children had been so hungry they could not sleep. They had heard all that their stepmother and father had said. Gretel wept bitterly, but Hansel said to her, "Do not weep. I will think of something to help us."

When all was still he got up, put on his coat, and crept out of the house. In the moonlight he could see some pebbles shining like silver in the path by the door. He filled his pockets with them and crept back to bed.

When morning came the two children were wakened by their stepmother saying,

"Get up, lazy bones, for we are going into the forest to work. Here is a piece of bread for each of you for your dinner."

Gretel carried the bread because Hansel's pockets were filled with pebbles. On their way to the forest Hansel stopped and looked back at the house so often that finally his father cried,

"What are you looking at, Hansel?"

"I am looking at my little white kitten, Father. She is sitting on the roof to wave me goodbye."

"You silly boy," said the woman, "that is not your kitten. That is the sun shining on the chimney."

Now every time Hansel stopped to look back at the house he had dropped a pebble from his pocket.

When they had walked a long, long way the father told the children to gather wood and he would make a fire. Hansel and Gretel gathered so much brushwood it made a small hill. Then the father set it on fire. When it burned brightly the stepmother said,

"Now children, lie down and rest. When we have finished our work we will come back for you."

So the children rested by the fire, thinking they heard their father chopping wood near by. But the noise they heard was not their father. It was a dry branch tapping against a dead tree. Soon they fell asleep. When they awoke it was night and they were all alone. Gretel began to cry.

"Wait, Gretel, don't cry. When the moon rises we can see the pebbles I dropped. Then we can find the way home."

When the moon rose they followed the path marked out by the stones. After walking all night long they came to their father's house. And oh, how glad he was to see them, for he had not wanted to leave his children in the forest.

But soon again there was not enough to eat and one night the children heard their stepmother say,

"Tomorrow we will take the children deeper into the forest where they have never been. This time they will not find the way back."

The father did not like this plan any better than he had the first one, but he had given in once so he had to give in a second time.

When all was still, Hansel got up to fill his pockets with pebbles. But the door was locked and he could not get out.

"Don't cry, Gretel. God will help us."

The next morning they again started for the forest. This time the wife gave each child only half a piece of bread. Hansel crumbled his bread and every now and then threw some on the ground. He stopped and looked back so often that his father said,

"Hansel what are you stopping for?"

"I am looking at my little white pigeon. She is sitting on the roof to wave goodbye to me."

"You silly boy," said the woman, "that is not your pigeon but the sun shining on the chimney."

They went farther into the wood this time. The father made a fire and again he and the stepmother left the children to rest by it.

Gretel gave half of her piece of bread to Hansel for he had dropped his along the path. Then the children fell asleep and when they awoke it was moonlight. They started to find their way home by the crumbs which Hansel had dropped, but they were not to be seen. The birds had eaten them.

Hansel and Gretel were frightened but they tried to find their way home without the breadcrumbs. They walked and they walked, but they could not see the way home. They got deeper and deeper into the woods. They were very hungry for they had nothing to eat but the few berries they found. The third morning in the woods they saw a little white bird. It sang such a sweet song that they followed it when it flew away. It led them to a little house. When they came near, they saw that the walls were made of bread, the roof was made of cakes, and the windows were made of sugar candy.

"You can have some of the window, Gretel, and I will take some of the roof." Hansel broke off a piece of the cake roof. Gretel started to bite the window. A voice called from inside the house.

> *"Nibble, nibble, like a mouse,*
> *Who is nibbling at my house?"*

The children called back,

> *"Never mind,*
> *It is the wind."*

They were so hungry they went right on eating. The door opened and out hobbled a little old woman on a crutch.

"Well, children dears, come inside. You must stay with me." And she took the two children into the house where they sat down to a good dinner of pancakes and milk, apples, sugar, and nuts.

After dinner, the old woman led Hansel and Gretel to two beautiful white beds. How comfortable they looked! The children had walked so far and were so tired they fell asleep in the beds at once. Now the old woman was really a witch. She looked at their rosy faces and said,

"What a fine feast they will make!"

In the morning she took Hansel to the stable and locked him in. she said to Gretel,

"Now, lazy bones, get up, bring some water and cook a nice breakfast for your brother. When he is fat enough I will eat him."

Cry as she might, Gretel had to do as she was told. She always had to cook good things for Hansel while she herself had little to eat.

Every morning the old witch said to the boy,

"Hold out your finger so that I may feel if you are fat enough." Now the old witch could not see very well so she did not know that Hansel held out a bone instead of his finger. Of course this felt very thin to the old woman. However, one morning the witch said,

> *"Be he fat or be he lean,*
> *Today I'll lick the platter clean,"*

and no matter how much Gretel cried she had to get wood and make a fire.

"First we will do the baking," said the witch. "The fire is burning so you, Gretel, crawl into the oven and see if it is hot enough to bake the bread."

But Gretel was afraid, for she knew the old woman meant to bake her. So she said,

"But I don't know how to get into the oven."

"You silly goose! This is the way to get in," and saying this the old woman put her head into the oven. Then Gretel gave the witch a big push. She pushed her so hard that the old witch fell head first into the oven. Gretel banged the iron door shut.

The wicked old witch would never eat any more children!

Gretel ran and let Hansel out. How happy they were to be free and to be together again. They danced and sang and kissed each other. They went into the witch's house and in every room they found jewels—pearls and diamonds and precious stones. Hansel filled his pockets and Gretel filled her apron with them, for they wanted to take their father a present.

But how to find their way home! They walked and walked and after a long time they came to a great lake. There was no bridge, but out on the water they saw a beautiful white duck.

"Duck, duck, here we stand
Hansel and Gretel on the land.
Boats and bridges do we lack
Will you not carry us on your back?"

And the duck swam to them and took Hansel first and then Gretel to the other side of the lake.

After that it was not far to their father's house. They flung open the door and rushed into their father's arms. And oh how glad he was to see them! His wife had died and he wanted his children more than ever! He had not been happy a minute since leaving them in the wood.

So Hansel and Gretel found their way home, safe and sound. Gretel opened her apron and Hansel emptied his pockets and the jewels fell over the floor. Their troubles were over and they lived happily together ever after.

Little Red Riding Hood

ONCE upon a time there lived a sweet little girl, who was loved by every one who knew her. On her birthday her grandmother gave her a lovely warm red cape with a hood of red velvet. The child liked it so much that she wore it everywhere. Soon every one called her Little Red Riding Hood.

One day her mother said, "You must go to see your grand-mother today. She has not been very well lately. You may take this basket to her. There is a loaf of bread and a little pot of butter in the basket." Little Red Riding Hood set out at once. Her grand-mother lived in a little white house on the other side of the wood.

Little Red Riding Hood was about halfway through the wood when she met a great big wolf.

"Good morning," said the wolf in a friendly voice. "Where are you going, little girl?"

"I am going to see my grandmother," said Little Red Riding

Hood. "She lives in the little white house on the other side of the wood. She has been sick, and I am taking her a loaf of bread and a little pot of butter in my basket."

"Wouldn't you like to take her some flowers, too?" said the wolf. "There are such pretty ones growing here."

Little Red Riding Hood began to pick some flowers for her grandmother at once. The wolf slipped away and ran as fast as he could to the grandmother's house. He knocked at the door.

"Who is there?" called the grandmother, from her bed.

"It is I, Little Red Riding Hood," said the wolf. He tried to make his voice sound like a little girl's. "I have brought you a loaf of bread and a little pot of butter that Mother just made."

"Then pull at the bobbin, lift up the latch, and walk in," said the grandmother.

So the wolf pulled at the bobbin and the door flew open. He rushed into the room and was going to eat up the grandmother, but she jumped out of bed and hid in a cupboard where the wolf could not reach her. Then the wolf shut the door, put on one of the grandmother's night caps, and jumped into bed to wait for Little Red Riding Hood.

It was not long before she tapped at the door and the wolf called out, "Who is there?"

"How funny Grandmother's voice sounds," thought the little girl. "But I suppose she has a bad cold."

"It is I, Little Red Riding Hood," she said. "I have brought you a loaf of bread and a little pot of butter that Mother just made."

"Then pull at the bobbin, lift up the latch, and walk in," said the wolf in the grandmother's voice.

So Little Red Riding Hood pulled at the bobbin and lifted the latch, and then she stepped inside the room.

"Put down the basket and come and talk to me," said the wolf.

So Little Red Riding Hood put the basket on the table.

"Oh, Grandmother!" she cried. "What great ears you have!"

"All the better to hear you with, my dear," said the wolf.

"But, Grandmother, what big eyes you have!"

"All the better to see you with, my dear."

"And, Grandmother, what a big nose you have!"

"All the better to smell you with, my dear," said the wolf.

"But, Grandmother, your mouth is so big, and your teeth are so sharp."

"All the better to eat you with, my dear!" said the wolf.

Then he sprang at poor Little Red Riding Hood, meaning to eat her up. But Little Red Riding Hood ran across the room toward the door. She screamed as loudly as she could.

Just then a young hunter happened to be passing the little white house. He stopped to see what was the matter.

When he saw the wolf, he came rushing to the door of the house and shot the wicked wolf straight through the heart.

"Where is Grandmother?" asked Little Red Riding Hood. "Oh, I do hope that the wolf has not eaten her, too."

At the sound of the shot, the cupboard door opened and the grandmother came out. Little Red Riding Hood ran to her arms, glad to see that she was not hurt a bit. The hunter carried the wolf away where he could not harm them any more, and Red Riding Hood and her mother and grandmother lived happily ever after.

The Magic City
of Children

TINKLE and Tommy were the only children on the island.
At least they didn't know any others. They were tired of
playing all alone. They wanted something to happen.
Suddenly something *did* happen!

Swoopity-swoop! a great shining thing flashed through the sky
and bounced at their feet.

"It's the magic ball!" they squealed gleefully, for it had led them
into adventures before.

"Run, Tinkle, run!" Tommy shouted. "It's going into the Tall
Dark Woods."

It went bounding ahead through the trees, guiding them straight
to the witch's little white house. And there was the jolly little old

lady herself, all dressed up in her funny bonnet and mittens as though she were going somewhere.

"Good morning, children," she beamed. "What a lovely day for visiting!"

"Good morning, Mrs. Erutan," they answered. "Are you going somewhere?"

"Oh, you're invited too!" she said quickly. "We'll visit some of my children. I have hundreds, and millions, and billions of them all together."

Then she picked a leaf. It grew, and it GREW, and it GREW. It got as big as a dinner table.

"All aboard!" she called, sitting on it. "Hold on tight!"

Whoooo-o-o! went the wind. Up went the leaf, swooping and dipping through the air.

"Oooo-o-o!" gasped the children. It was a long, long time before they dared to peek. Then, at last, they saw below them a ring of the cutest, prettiest, strangest, little houses in all the world.

The leaf fluttered down right in the middle of the circle.

"The houses are all just the right size!" laughed Tinkle, clapping her hands.

"Of course," nodded Mrs. Erutan, busily winding a huge watch, which she had borrowed from old Father Time. She must have been winding it backwards, for the sun went slippity-sliding all the way back to sunrise.

"Now we can begin at the beginning," she twinkled. "But which house will be the first?"

They were all so cute the children just couldn't decide, so Tommy counted, "Eeny-meeny-miney-mo . . ."

It was the little Hungarian house, and the tiny door opened before they even knocked.

"Come in!" called a little voice in Hungarian, which the children could suddenly understand very well.

"Aren't you coming in too?" Tommy asked Mrs. Erutan, but she shook her head.

She didn't like to admit that she couldn't get through the door. She just said she had a lot to attend to leaving her calling cards all around. "It's sociable," she said, "and besides it reminds them not to spell my name backwards." (Can you guess what it spells that way?)

So the children stepped into the little house alone. It was very dark inside, for there were no windows, but they could dimly see the furniture. In the corner of the room was a funny mud stove looking like a great white pear with a shelf around it for people to sit on. And there was the little Hungarian boy himself.

"My, you're dressed up!" said Tinkle admiringly. He looked as though he had on skirts, but they were really trousers.

"Everybody here wears pretty clothes," said the little Hungarian boy.

Then he showed them his farm where everything was exactly the right size too. The cow was only as big as a calf. The mother pig was the

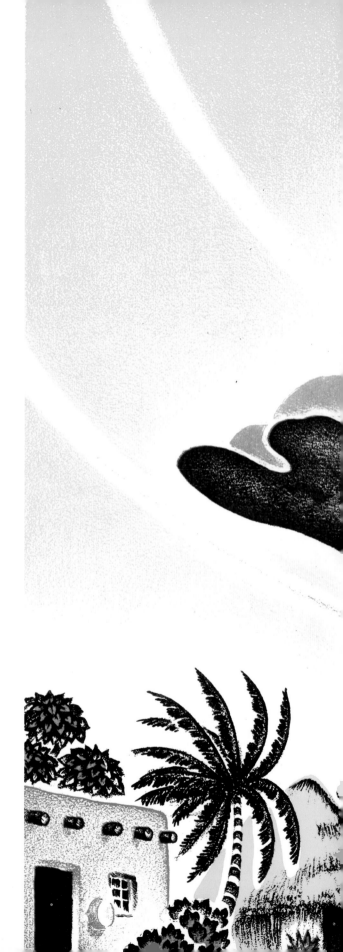

size of a puppy. The piglets were no bigger than mice. And the geese looked like pigeons.

Then oh! what a good time they had. It was so much fun to milk the tiny cow and the little Hungarian boy let them take turns. It was like a game finding the wee little goose eggs, and feeding all the hungry little animals. But Tinkle and Tommy and the little Hungarian boy were the hungriest of all.

They hurried back to the house and made the nicest omelets. My! how they disappeared! And goodness what a lot of milk they drank!

They would have stayed all day, but Mrs. Erutan called them. So they thanked the little Hungarian boy, and sadly told him goodbye.

"It's your turn now, Tinkle," said Mrs. Erutan. "Which house do you choose?"

So Tinkle counted like Tommy. This time it was the little Hawaiian house.

The funny little house was made of grass, with a thick pointed roof that sloped four ways. It was shaded by palms and had no windows at all. It must have been very dark inside.

Before they could knock, a pretty little Hawaiian girl appeared in the doorway.

"Welcome!" she said in Hawaiian, which they could suddenly understand very well.

She was holding wreaths of flowers which she had made herself. There was a little wreath to hang around Tinkle's neck. And another little one for Tommy. And a great BIG one for Mrs. Erutan. The little Hawaiian girl must have known they were coming.

"Let's all go swimming!" she cried suddenly, dancing and clapping her hands at the thought.

"Where's the water?" asked Tommy eagerly.

"But we haven't any bathing suits," mourned Tinkle.

"I'll get some!" promised the little Hawaiian girl, dashing back into the house.

Then she brought a little bathing suit for Tinkle. And another little one for Tommy. And a great BIG one for Mrs. Erutan.

Behind the house, by the pineapple garden, was a little path that ran straight to the sea.

Then there was one little splash. And another. And another. And a great BIG splash!

All the little fishes came to join in the fun. And what a noisy, splashy, spluttery, merry time everybody had!

The little Hawaiian girl was as graceful as a fish, and very brave. She could stand on a board, without holding on, and go skimming over the waves to the beach.

"Let me try!" Tommy cried.

"Show me how!" begged Tinkle.

Oh, they would have liked to stay there all day long. At last Mrs. Erutan got out of the water, and so did the little Hawaiian girl, but Tinkle and Tommy kept right on swimming.

"There won't be any time left!" warned Mrs. Erutan.

Then Tinkle and Tommy dressed, thanked the little Hawaiian girl, and very sadly told her goodbye.

"Now where do you think you'll like to have lunch?" Mrs. Erutan asked the children.

It was Tommy's turn again, and this time he counted out on the little Mexican house.

It was made of adobe mud, and set in a bright flower garden under a cottonwood tree. Behind it were tiny gold and purple mountains. The air was dry, and hot, and smelling of flowers.

Before the children could knock, the little door opened, and there stood the smiling little Mexican girl.

"You are most welcome," she said in Spanish, which they could suddenly understand very well.

She took them into a tiny low room. The floor was made of dirt, and the ceiling was made of poles with sticks laid across. The little furniture was brightly painted with flowers, and strings of corn and peppers hung from the whitewashed walls.

Tiny pet animals and birds were running and flying all around the room. And what a noise of squealings, and cluckings, and barkings, and gruntings, and chatterings they made!

"They're hungry," said the little Mexican girl, feeding chili and cheese to the fussy baby mocking birds.

The children were getting hungry too. So when they had helped to feed all the animals, they began to fix lunch for themselves.

The little Mexican girl showed Tinkle how to grind corn with stones and pat the meal into little cakes called *tortillas*. Tommy learned to make *tamales* out of cornmeal and meat. He wrapped them in corn shucks like neat little packages, while the little Mexican girl stirred a pot of beans and chili.

At last they took everything into the garden, and Mrs. Erutan was so surprised and pleased to be invited to the party. The children had felt on fire inside, but they liked the hot chili just the same. They liked the little Mexican girl. They liked her house, and the way she lived with all her pets. They would have liked to stay there all day long, but Mrs. Erutan said they must leave. So they thanked the little Mexican girl and sadly told her goodbye.

"Which house shall it be this afternoon?" wondered Mrs. Erutan.

It was Tinkle's turn again. She counted, and this time it was the little Chinese house. It was a very grand little house made of tiles, with tiny courts and gardens. Some of the gates were moon-shaped, or shaped like vases and lutes.

Before they could knock the door opened, and the little Chinese boy was smiling and bowing them into his house. He was also making polite speeches in

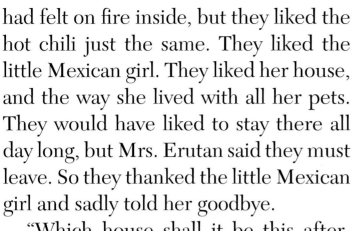

Chinese, which they could suddenly understand very well. He was the most polite boy they had ever met.

He took Tinkle and Tommy through his house and showed them all his toys. Best of all were the wonderful kites. They were made like birds, and animals, and men. Tinkle and Tommy had never seen anything like them.

"But you need a wind for flying kites," smiled Mrs. Erutan, peeking over the top of the wall.

93

And, *Whooo-o-o!* There was the wind blowing as nice as you please.

The little Chinese boy welcomed Mrs. Erutan so gladly that soon she was flying a kite too. Before long the little Persian boy, and the little Korean boy, and the little Japanese boy saw the kites flying, and came bringing their own.

Then they had the most wonderful battle, flying kites the Persian way. The little Persian boy had brought some ground glass paste to rub on the kite strings. As the kites flew around, everybody tried to use his string to saw another string in two. Then how they squealed, and shouted, and ran to catch a kite when it came fluttering down.

It was so much fun that Tommy and Tinkle would have liked to fly kites all day long. But Mrs. Erutan said they must go, though she liked to fly kites herself.

When the little Chinese boy told them goodbye, he gave them each a present. Tommy's was a beautiful kite painted like a fish. And Tinkle's was lovely too, but hers was like a bird.

So they thanked the little Chinese boy, and sadly told all the boys goodbye.

"Now, which house?" asked Mrs. Erutan.

"Eeny-meeny-miney-mo . . ." counted Tommy. It was the little Dutch house. Mrs. Erutan said she would meet them in the garden.

The little Dutch house had a funny roof made partly of tiles and partly of thatch. The bottom half of the door was closed, but the top half was open, and a pretty little Dutch girl was peeking out at them.

"Good afternoon!" she said in Dutch, which the children could suddenly understand very well.

Then she welcomed them into a low squatty room with tall narrow furniture. Everything gleamed, from the tiny copper pots, to the blue Dutch tiles on the fireplace.

Afterwards she took them to the back of her little house. The

land was flat as far as they could see, and dotted with tiny wind-mills. Tulips were growing everywhere, and all around were little silver canals, sparkling in the sun.

It was lovely, but the little Dutch girl just sighed. "If it were only winter," she said, "we could all go skating."

"And why not?" twinkled Mrs. Erutan, doing some magic that made winter come in a minute.

"Brrr-r-r!" shivered Tinkle.

Tommy flapped his arms.

The little Dutch girl raced back to the house and brought them some warm Dutch clothes. She brought three pairs of little skates and one pair of BIG ones, so they all could go skating on the tiny canals.

They skated and skated. What fun it was! And how they laughed to see Mrs. Erutan spinning like a top. The little Dutch girl could skate like a fairy. Tinkle and Tommy were learning fast, too. It couldn't matter if Tinkle did fall down once or twice. With so many petticoats on she could hardly feel the bumps. How they shouted as they skated about! And what a merry time they had playing lash-the-whip!

The children would gladly have skated all day, but at last Mrs. Erutan said they must go. Then she wound the watch, and spring came scurrying back again. So they thanked the little Dutch girl and sadly told her goodbye.

It was supper time by then.

"I'm having dinner with the little French girl," said Mrs. Erutan.

Tommy said he would very much rather see the Eskimo house.

It was made of ice and looked like a bowl upside down. The only door was a tunnel of ice, and it was full of dogs called "huskies."

"Come in!" called a little voice, speaking Eskimo, which they could suddenly understand very well.

The little Eskimo boy lent them some warm Eskimo clothes, and they all went out again, and hitched the huskies to a sled.

"Mush!" cried the little Eskimo boy to the dogs, meaning, "Get up!"

He took hold behind the sled, and away they went over the snow and ice.

After a while he stopped to make a hole in the ice, and they fished until Tinkle caught a herring.

"Mush," he said again, and they came to another hole. Then he showed them how to catch a seal.

"Mush!" he said for the third time. But this time Tinkle and Tommy had to walk because the seal was on the sled.

They walked and walked, and suddenly Tommy shot a polar bear. They put him on the sled too.

The little Eskimo boy said, "Mush!" for the last time, and they went straight back to the *igloo*. "It's time for supper," he said at last, giving them each a piece of raw herring. Tinkle and Tommy could have eaten a bear, but they just couldn't eat raw fish.

Next the little Eskimo boy gave them some strips of raw seal fat. He called it "blubber" and said it tasted fine. But Tinkle and Tommy thought they'd rather starve. It began to look as though they would. They wondered what Mrs. Erutan was having for supper, but that only made things worse.

Finally the little Eskimo boy skinned the bear and cooked it. So Tinkle and Tommy really did eat a bear, and they were so terribly hungry it tasted wonderful.

Then Mrs. Erutan called them away, so they thanked the little Eskimo boy, and sadly told him goodbye.

"It's late. You'd better go home now," said Mrs. Erutan.

"Oh!" gasped the children. "What will Mother say?"

"Never mind," smiled Mrs. Erutan, "I'll fix the watch, and you'll get home so long ago she'll never even worry."

She sat on the big leaf again, calling, "Hurry! All aboard! Hold on tight!" And up it rose into the air.

Whooo-o-o! Away flew Tommy's kite. It pulled him right off the leaf.

Whoooo-o-o! Another wind caught Tinkle's, pulling her after him.

"Goodbye!" called Mrs. Erutan.

"Goodbye!" they shouted back, not feeling at all afraid.

Every minute it grew earlier. The sun backed up the sky. They were home again by supper time.

"I'm afraid we're not hungry," Tommy explained. "Tinkle and I just ate a bear."

"Why, Tommy!" his mother said. "Aren't you ashamed? You know you never ate a bear."

But Tinkle and Tommy giggled because they knew they had.

Mother Goose
Her Best-Known Rhymes

WEE WILLIE WINKIE

Wee Willie Winkie runs through the town,
Upstairs and downstairs in his nightgown;
Tapping at the window, crying at the lock,
"Are the babies in their bed? for it's now
    ten o'clock."

WHOOP! RING THE BELLS

Whoop! Ring the bells, and
    sound the drums,
Tomorrow school vacation
    comes.

MONDAY'S CHILD

Monday's child is fair of face,
Tuesday's child is full of grace,
Wednesday's child is full of woe,
Thursday's child has far to go,
Friday's child is loving and giving,
Saturday's child works hard for its living;
And a child that is born on Christmasday
Is fair, and wise, and good, and gay.

LITTLE MISS MUFFET

Little Miss Muffet sat on a
    tuffet,
Eating of curds and whey;
There came a big spider,
    and sat down beside her,
And frightened Miss
    Muffet away.

RIDE A COCK-HORSE

Ride a cock-horse to Banbury
    Cross,
To see a fine lady upon a white
    horse!
Rings on her fingers, and bells on
    her toes,
She shall make music wherever
    she goes.

TO MARKET, TO MARKET

To market, to market, to buy a
    plum bun,
Home again, home again, market
    is done.

DAFFY-DOWN-DILLY

Daffy-Down-Dilly has come up
    to town,
In a yellow petticoat and a green
    gown.

WHERE ARE YOU GOING, MY PRETTY MAID

"Where are you going, my pretty maid?"
"I'm going a-milking, sir," she said.

"May I go with you, my pretty maid?"
"You're kindly welcome, sir," she said.

"What is your father, my pretty maid?"
"My father's a farmer, sir," she said.

"What is your fortune, my pretty
    maid?"
"My face is my fortune,
    sir," she said.

"Then I can't marry
    you, my pretty
    maid!"
"Nobody asked you,
    sir!" she said.

RUB-A-DUB-DUB

Rub-a-dub-dub, three men in a tub,
The butcher, the baker, the candlestick maker;
And they all jumped over a hot potato.

PUSSY-CAT, PUSSY-CAT

Pussy-cat, pussy-cat,
Where have you been?
I've been to London
To look at the Queen.

Pussy-cat, pussy-cat,
What did you there?
I frightened a little mouse
Under the chair.

THERE WAS A CROOKED MAN

There was a crooked man, and he went a crooked mile,
He found a crooked sixpence against a crooked stile;
He bought a crooked cat, which caught a crooked mouse,
And they all lived together in a little crooked house.

SEE-SAW, MARGERY DAW

See-saw, Margery Daw,
Johnny shall have a new master,
He shall have but a penny a day,
Because he can't work any faster.

OLD MOTHER HUBBARD

Old Mother Hubbard
Went to the cupboard,
To get her poor dog a bone;
But when she came there,
The cupboard was bare,
And so the poor dog had none.

She went to the baker's
To buy him some bread;
But when she came back,
The poor dog was dead.

She went to the joiner's
To buy him a coffin;
But when she came back,
The poor dog was laughing.

She went to the hatter's
To buy him a hat;
But when she came back,
He was feeding the cat.

She went to the barber's
To buy him a wig;
But when she came back,
He was dancing a jig.

She went to the tailor's
To buy him a coat;
But when she came back,
He was riding a goat.

She went to the cobbler's
To buy him some shoes;
But when she came back,
He was reading the news.

She went to the hosier's
To buy him some hose;
But when she came back,
He was dressed in his clothes.

The dame made a curtsy,
The dog made a bow;
The dame said, "Your servant,"
The dog said, "Bow wow."

THE GREEDY MAN

A greedy man is he who sits
And bites bits off the plates;
And then takes down the
   calendars
And gobbles up the dates.

CURLY LOCKS

Curly Locks, Curly Locks,
Wilt thou be mine?
Thou shalt not wash dishes,
Nor yet feed the swine;
But sit on a cushion,
And sew a fine seam,
And feed upon strawberries,
Sugar and cream.

LITTLE BOY BLUE

Little Boy Blue, come blow your
    horn,
The sheep's in the meadow, the
    cow's in the corn;
Where's the little boy that looks
    after the sheep?
He's under the haycock, fast
    asleep.
Go wake him, go wake him.
Oh! no, not I;
For if I wake him, he'll certainly
    cry.

ONE, HE LOVES

One, he loves; two, he loves;
Three, he loves, they say;
Four, he loves with all his heart;
Five, he casts away.
Six, he loves; seven, she loves;
Eight, they both love.
Nine, he comes; ten, he tarries;
Eleven, he courts; twelve, he
    marries.

A WALNUT

As soft as silk, as white as milk,
As bitter as gall, a strong wall,
And a green coat covers me all.

I SAW A SHIP A-SAILING

I saw a ship a-sailing,
A-sailing on the sea;
And it was full of pretty things
For baby and for me.

There were comfits in the cabin,
And apples in the hold;
The sails were all of velvet,
And the masts of beaten gold.

The four-and-twenty sailors
That stood between the decks
Were four-and-twenty white
    mice,
With chains about their necks.

The captain was a duck,
With a packet on his back;
And when the ship began to
    move,
The captain said, "Quack! Quack!"

TO BABYLON

How many miles is it to
    Babylon?—
Three score miles and ten.
Can I get there by candlelight?—
Yes, and back again;
If your heels are nimble and light,
You may get there by candlelight.

TOM, TOM, THE PIPER'S SON

Tom, Tom, the Piper's son,
Stole a pig and away did run.
The pig was eaten, and Tom was beaten,
And Tom went roaring down the street.

COME, LET'S TO BED

Come, let's to bed, says Sleepy-head;
Tarry awhile, says Slow;
Put on the pan, says Greedy Nan,
Let's sup before we go.

SUMMER BREEZE

Summer breeze, so
    softly blowing,
In my garden pinks are
    growing;
If you go and send the
    showers,
You may come and
    smell my flowers.

ONE, TWO, BUCKLE MY SHOE

One, two, buckle my shoe;
Three, four, shut the door;
Five, six, pick up sticks;
Seven, eight, lay them straight;
Nine, ten, a good fat hen;
Eleven, twelve, dig and delve;
Thirteen, fourteen, maids a-courting;
Fifteen, sixteen, maids in the kitchen;
Seventeen, eighteen, maids a-waiting;
Nineteen, twenty, my plate's empty.

I LOVE MY LITTLE KITTEN

I love my little kitten,
Her coat is so warm,
And if I don't hurt her,
She'll do me no harm.

So I'll not pull her tail,
Nor drive her away,
But kitty and I
Very gently will play.

LITTLE POLLY FLINDERS

Little Polly Flinders
Sat among the cinders,
Warming her pretty little toes!
Her mother came and caught her,
And punished her little daughter,
For spoiling her nice new clothes.

TAFFY WAS A WELSHMAN

Taffy was a Welshman, Taffy
was a thief;
Taffy came to my house and
stole a piece of beef.
I went to Taffy's house, Taffy
was not at home;
Taffy came to my house, and
stole a marrow-bone.
I went to Taffy's house, Taffy
was in bed;
I took the marrow-bone and
threw it at his head.

MARY, MARY

Mary, Mary, quite contrary,
How does your garden grow?
Silver bells and cockle-shells
And pretty maids all in a row.

THE MAN IN THE MOON

The man in the moon
   came tumbling down,
And asked the way to
   Norwich;
He went to the South
   and burnt his mouth,
With supping cold pease
   porridge.

WHEN THE WIND IS IN THE EAST

When the wind is in the east,
'Tis neither good for man nor beast;
When the wind is in the north,
The skilful fisher goes not forth;
When the wind is in the south,
It blows the bait in the fish's mouth;
When the wind is in the west,
Then 'tis at its very best.

PLUM PUDDING

Flour of England, fruit of Spain,
Met together in a shower of rain;
Put in a bag, tied round with a string;
If you'll tell me this riddle, I'll give you a ring.

SUNSHINE

Hick-a-more,
   Hack-a-more
On the King's kitchen
   door;
All the King's horses,
And all the King's men
Couldn't drive Hick-a-
   more, Hack-a-more
Off the King's kitchen
   door!

LITTLE ROBIN REDBREAST

Little Robin Redbreast
Sat upon a rail;
Niddle naddle went his head,
Wiggle waggle went his tail.

NEEDLES AND PINS

Needles and pins, needles
    and pins,
When a man marries his
    trouble begins.

SING A SONG OF SIXPENCE

Sing a song of sixpence,
A pocket full of rye;
Four-and-twenty blackbirds
Baked in a pie.

When the pie was opened,
The birds began to sing;
Was not that a dainty dish
To set before the King?

The King was in the counting house,
Counting out his money;
The Queen was in the parlor,
Eating bread and honey;

The maid was in the garden,
Hanging out the clothes;
There came by a blackbird,
And pecked off her nose.

ROCK-A-BYE, BABY

Rock-a-bye, baby, thy cradle
    is green;
Father's a nobleman,
    mother's a queen;
And Betty's a lady, and wears
    a gold ring;
And Johnny's a drummer, and
    drums for the King.

Rock-a-bye, baby, on the tree
    top,
When the wind blows, the
    cradle will rock.
When the bough breaks, the
    cradle will fall—
Down will come baby, cradle,
    and all.

BARBER, BARBER

Barber, barber, shave a pig;
How many hairs to make
   a wig?
Four-and-twenty, that's
   enough;
Give the poor barber a
   pinch of snuff.

A SUNSHINY SHOWER

A sunshiny shower
Won't last half an hour.

MARY HAD A LITTLE LAMB

Mary had a little lamb,
Its fleece was white as snow;
And everywhere that Mary went,
The lamb was sure to go.

He followed her to school one day;
That was against the rule;
It made the children laugh and play
To see a lamb at school.

And so the teacher turned him out,
But still he lingered near,
And waited patiently about
Till Mary did appear.

Then he ran up to her, and laid
His head upon her arm
As if he said, "I'm not afraid—
You'll keep me from all harm."

"What makes the lamb love Mary so?"
The eager children cry.
"Oh, Mary loves the lamb, you know,"
The teacher did reply.

And you each gentle animal
In confidence may bind,
And make them follow at your will
If you are only kind.

OLD MOTHER TWITCHETT

Old Mother Twitchett
  had but one eye,
And a long tail which
  she let fly;
And every time she
  went over a gap,
She left a bit of her tail
  in a trap.
(A needle and thread)

BYE, BABY BUNTING

Bye, baby bunting,
Daddy's gone a-hunting
To get a little rabbit skin
To wrap the baby
  bunting in.

LITTLE BO-PEEP

Little Bo-Peep has lost her sheep
And can't tell where to find them;
Leave them alone and they'll come home,
And bring their tails behind them.

Little Bo-Peep fell fast asleep,
And dreamed she heard them bleating;
But when she awoke, she found it a joke,
For still they were a-fleeting.

Then up she took her little crook,
Determined for to find them;
She found them, indeed, but it made her
  heart bleed,
For they'd left their tails behind them.

It happened one day, as Bo-Peep did stray
Upon a meadow hard by,
There she espied their tails side by side,
All hung on a tree to dry.

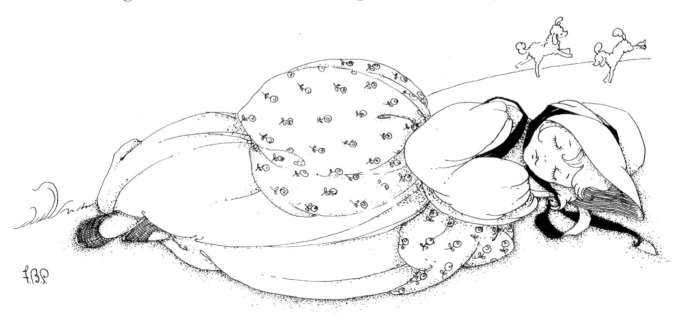

I HAD A LITTLE PONY

I had a little pony,
His name was Dapple-gray;
I lent him to a lady,
To ride a mile away;
She whipped him, she slashed him,
She rode him through the mire;
I would not lend my pony more
For all the lady's hire.

THREE WISE MEN

Three wise men of Gotham
Went to sea in a bowl;
And if the bowl had been stronger
My story would have been longer.

IT COSTS LITTLE GOSSIP

It costs Little Gossip her income
　for shoes,
To travel about and carry the news.

A CHERRY

As I went through the garden gap,
Whom should I meet but Dick
　Red-cap!
A stick in his hand, a stone in his
　throat.
If you tell me this riddle, I'll give
　you a groat.

A CANDLE

Little Nannie Etticoat,
In a white petticoat,
The longer she stands,
The shorter she grows.

PETER PIPER

Peter Piper picked a peck of
　pickled peppers;
A peck of pickled peppers
　Peter Piper picked.
If Peter Piper picked a peck of
　pickled peppers,
Where's the peck of pickled
　peppers Peter Piper picked?

THERE WAS A LITTLE GIRL

There was a little girl
And she wore a little curl
Right down the middle of
  her forehead.
When she was good,
She was very, very good,
But when she was
  naughty, she was
  horrid.

BUTTERFLY, BUTTERFLY

Butterfly, butterfly, whence do you come?
I know not; I ask not; I never had a home.

Butterfly, butterfly, where do you go?
Where the sun shines, and where the
  buds grow.

THE WAVES NEVER SLEEP

The waves never sleep—
By night and by day
They leap and they dance,
They tumble and play,
And sing a sweet song;
But what do they say?

GOOSEY, GOOSEY, GANDER

Goosey, goosey, gander,
Whither do you wander?
Upstairs, and downstairs;
And in my lady's
  chamber.
There I met an old man,
Who would not say his
  prayers;
I took him by his left leg
And threw him down the
  stairs.

THE QUEEN OF HEARTS

The Queen of Hearts, she
    made some tarts,
All on a summer's day;
The Knave of Hearts, he stole
    the tarts,
And took them right away.

The King of Hearts called for
    the tarts,
And beat the Knave full sore;
The Knave of Hearts brought
    back the tarts,
And vowed he'd steal no more.

HICKETY, PICKETY

Hickety, pickety, my black hen,
She lays eggs for gentlemen;
Gentlemen come every day
To see what my black hen
    doth lay.

A DILLER, A DOLLAR

A diller, a dollar, a ten-o'clock
    scholar,
What makes you come so soon?
You used to come at ten o'clock,
And now you come at noon.

THE LION AND THE UNICORN

The lion and the unicorn
Were fighting for the crown!
The lion beat the unicorn
All round about the town.

And some gave them brown;
Some gave them plum-cake,
And sent them out of town.

JACK SPRATT

Jack Spratt could eat no fat,
His wife could eat no lean;
And so between them both
They left the platter clean.

HEY! DIDDLE, DIDDLE

Hey! diddle, diddle, the cat and the fiddle,
The cow jumped over the moon;
The little dog laughed to see such sport;
And the dish ran away with the spoon.

HUMPTY DUMPTY

Humpty Dumpty sat on a wall,
Humpty Dumpty had a great fall,
All the King's horses and all the
    King's men
Could not put Humpty Dumpty
    together again.

THE YEAR

January brings the snow,
Makes our feet and fingers glow.

February brings the rain,
Thaws the frozen lake again.

March brings breezes loud and shrill,
Stirs the dancing daffodil.

April brings the primrose sweet,
Scatters daisies at our feet.

May brings flocks of pretty lambs,
Skipping by their fleecy dams.

June brings tulips, lilies, roses,
Fills the children's hands with posies.

Hot July brings cooling showers,
Apricots and gillyflowers.

August brings the sheaves of corn,
Then the harvest home is borne.

Warm September brings the fruit;
Sportsmen then begin to shoot.

Fresh October brings the pheasant;
Then to gather nuts is pleasant.

Dull November brings the blast,
Then the leaves are whirling fast.

Chill December brings the sleet,
Blazing fire and Christmas treat.

THE NORTH WIND DOTH BLOW

The north wind doth blow,
And we shall have snow,
And what will the robin
   do then,
Poor thing?

He will sit in the barn
And keep himself warm,
And hide his head under
   his wing,
Poor thing!

WHEN I WAS
A LITTLE BOY

When I was a little boy,
I lived by myself,
And all the bread and cheese
   I got
I put upon the shelf.

The rats and mice
They led me such a life,
I was forced to go to
   London town
To buy me a wife.

The streets were so broad,
And the lanes were so narrow,
I could not get my wife home
In a wheelbarrow.

The wheelbarrow broke,
And my wife got a fall,
Down came the wheelbarrow,
Wife and all.

HANDY SPANDY

Handy Spandy, Jack-a-dandy,
Loved plum-cake and sugar candy;
He bought some at a grocer's shop,
And out he came, hop, hop, hop.

LITTLE MAIDEN

Little maiden, better tarry;
Time enough next year to
   marry.
Hearts may change, and so
   may fancy;
Wait a little longer, Nancy.

PETER, PETER

Peter, Peter, pumpkin-eater,
Had a wife, and couldn't keep her;
He put her in a pumpkin-shell,
And there he kept her very well.

Peter, Peter, pumpkin-eater,
Had another and didn't love her;
Peter learned to read and spell,
And then he loved her very well.

HICKORY, DICKORY, DOCK

Hickory, dickory, dock,
The mouse ran up the clock,
The clock struck one,
The mouse ran down;
Hickory, dickory, dock.

LOVELY RAINBOW

Lovely rainbow, hung so high,
Quite across the distant sky,
Please touch the ground close by my side,
And o'er your bridge I'll pony ride.

SEE A PIN AND PICK IT UP

See a pin and pick it up,
And all the day you'll have good luck;
See a pin and let it lay,
Bad luck you'll have all the day!

JOCKY WAS A PIPER'S SON

Jocky was a piper's son,
And he fell in love when
he was young;
And the only tune he
could play
Was "Over the hills and
far away;"
Over the hills and a great
way off,
And the wind will blow
my top-knot off.

PACE, PACE, MY LADY

Pace, pace, my lady, never
drive fast,
Ride very slowly, daylight
will last;
The day is so pleasant, the
breeze is so bracing,
That looking at Nature is
better than racing.

Pace, pace, my lady, never
drive fast,
Ride very slowly, daylight
will last;
The world is so fair, the
breeze is so bracing,
That looking at Nature is
better than racing.

BOBBIE SHAFTOE

Bobbie Shaftoe's gone to sea,
Silver buckles at his knee;
When he comes back, he'll
    marry me,
Bonny Bobbie Shaftoe!

Bobbie Shaftoe has a cow,
Black and white about the
    mow;
Open the gates and let her
    through,
Bobbie Shaftoe's ain cow!

Bobbie Shaftoe has a hen,
Cockle button, cockle ben,
She lays eggs for gentlemen,
But none for Bobbie Shaftoe!

A LITTLE BIRD

Once I saw a little bird
Come hop, hop, hop;
So I cried, "Little bird,
Will you stop, stop, stop?"
And was going to the window
To say, "How do you do?"
But he shook his little tail,
And far away he flew.

IF "IF'S" AND "AND'S"

If "if's" and "and's" were pots and pans,
There'd be no need for tinkers' hands!

TEARS AND FEARS

Tommy's tears and Mary's fears
Will make them old before their years.

FOR WANT OF A NAIL

For want of a nail, the shoe
    was lost,
For want of the shoe, the
    horse was lost,
For want of the horse, the
    rider was lost,
For want of the rider, the
    battle was lost,
For want of the battle, the
    kingdom was lost,
And all for the want of a
    horseshoe nail!

THE OLD WOMAN OF HARROW

There was an old woman of
    Harrow,
Who visited in a wheelbarrow;
And her servant before
Knocked loud at
    each door,
To announce
    the old woman
    of Harrow.

I HAD A LITTLE HUSBAND

I had a little husband,
No bigger than my thumb;
I put him in a tiny pot,
And there I bid him drum.

I bought a little horse,
That galloped up and down;
I bridled him, and saddled him,
And sent him out of town.

I gave him some garters,
To garter up his hose,
And a little pocket handkerchief
To wipe his pretty nose.

POLLY, PUT THE KETTLE ON

Polly, put the kettle on,
Polly, put the kettle on,
Polly, put the kettle on,
And we'll all have tea.

Sukey, take it off again,
Sukey, take it off again,
Sukey, take it off again,
And we'll all run away.

I SING, I SING

I sing, I sing from morn till night,
From cares I'm free, and my heart
    is light.

SIMPLE SIMON

Simple Simon met a pieman
Going to the fair;
Says Simple Simon to the pieman,
"Pray give me of your ware."

Says the pieman to Simple Simon,
"Show me first your penny."
Says Simple Simon to the pieman,
"Indeed I have not any."

Simple Simon went to see
If plums grew on a thistle;
He pricked his fingers very much,
Which made poor Simon whistle.

Simple Simon went a-fishing
For to catch a whale;
All the water he had got
Was in his mother's pail.

DING DONG BELL

Ding dong bell, pussy's in the
    well!
Who put her in?—Little
    Johnny Green.
Who pulled her out?—Little
    Tommy Trout.
What a naughty boy was that,
To drown poor pussy cat,
Who never did him any harm,
But killed the mice in his
    father's barn.

OLD KING COLE

Old King Cole
Was a merry old soul,
And a merry old soul was he.

He called for his pipe,
And he called for his bowl,
And he called for his fiddlers
    three.

Every fiddler, he had a fiddle,
And a very fine fiddle had he;
Twee tweedle dee, tweedle
    dee, went the fiddlers.

Oh, there's none so rare
As can compare
With King Cole and his
    fiddlers three.

OLD MOTHER GOOSE

Old Mother Goose, when
She wanted to wander,
Would ride through the air
On a very fine gander.

Mother Goose had a house,
'Twas built in a wood,
Where an owl at the door
For sentinel stood.

This is her son Jack,
A plain-looking lad;
He is not very good,
Nor yet very bad.

She sent him to market,
A live goose he bought.
"Here, mother," said he,
"It will not go for naught."

Jack's goose and her gander
Grew very fond;
They'd both eat together
Or swim in one pond.

Jack found one morning,
As I have been told,
His goose had laid him
An egg of pure gold.

Jack rode to his mother,
The news for to tell;
She called him a good boy
And said it was well.

Then Jack went a-courting
A lady so gay,
As fair as the lily,
And sweet as the May.

But then the old Squire
Came behind his back,
And began to belabor
The sides of poor Jack.

Then old Mother Goose
That instant came in,
And turned her son Jack
Into famed Harlequin.

She then, with her wand,
Touched the lady so fine
And turned her at once
Into sweet Columbine.

The gold egg in the sea
Was thrown away then,—
When Jack jumped in,
And got it back again.

Jack's mother came by,
And caught the goose soon,
And mounting its back,
Flew up to the moon.

LITTLE TOM TUCKER

Little Tom Tucker
Sings for his supper;
What shall he eat?
White bread and butter.
How shall he cut it
Without e'er a knife?
How can he marry
Without e'er a wife?

THERE WAS AN OLD WOMAN TOSSED UP IN A BASKET

There was an old woman tossed up
    in a basket,
Seventy times as high as the moon.
Where was she going? I couldn't
    but ask it,
For in her hand she carried a broom.

"Old woman, old woman, old
    woman," quoth I,
"Oh, whither, oh, whither, oh,
    whither so high?"
"To brush the cobwebs off the sky!
And I will be back again by-and-by."

LITTLE JACK HORNER

Little Jack Horner sat in a
    corner,
Eating a Christmas pie;
He put in his thumb, and
    pulled out a plum,
And said, "What a good boy
    am I!"

PEASE PORRIDGE HOT

Pease porridge hot,
Pease porridge cold,
Pease porridge in the pot,
Nine days old.
Spell me that without a P,
And a scholar you will be.
(*T-h-a-t*)

BOW-WOW, SAYS THE DOG

Bow-wow, says the dog;
Mew-mew, says the cat;
Grunt, grunt, goes the hog;
And squeak, goes the rat.
Tu-whu, says the owl;
Caw, caw, says the crow;
Quack, quack, says the duck;
And what sparrows say you know.
So with sparrows and owls,
With rats and with dogs,
With ducks and with crows,
With cats and with hogs,
A fine song I have made,
To please you, my dear;
And if it's well sung,
'Twill be charming to hear.

PAT-A-CAKE, PAT-A-CAKE

Pat-a-cake, pat-a-cake, baker's
    man,
So I will, master, as fast as I can,
Pat it, and prick it, and mark it
    with B,
Put it in the oven for baby and
    me.

COFFEE AND TEA

Molly, my sister, and I fell out,
And what do you think it was all
    about?
She loved coffee and I loved tea,
And that was the reason we
    couldn't agree.

JUMPING JOAN

Here am I, little
 jumping Joan;
When nobody's with
 me, I'm always alone.

COCK CROWS IN THE MORN

Cock crows in the morn
 to tell us to rise,
And he who lies late will
 never be wise:
For early to bed and
 early to rise,
Is the way to be healthy,
 wealthy and wise.

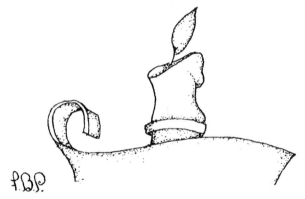

THREE BLIND MICE

Three blind mice, see
 how they run!
They all ran after the
 farmer's wife,
She cut off their tails
 with a carving knife;
Did you ever hear such
 a thing in your life?
Three blind mice.

JACK BE NIMBLE

Jack be nimble, Jack be quick;
Jack jump over the candle-stick.

FOR EVERY EVIL

For every evil under the sun
There is a remedy, or there is none.
If there be one, try to find it.
If there be none, never mind it.

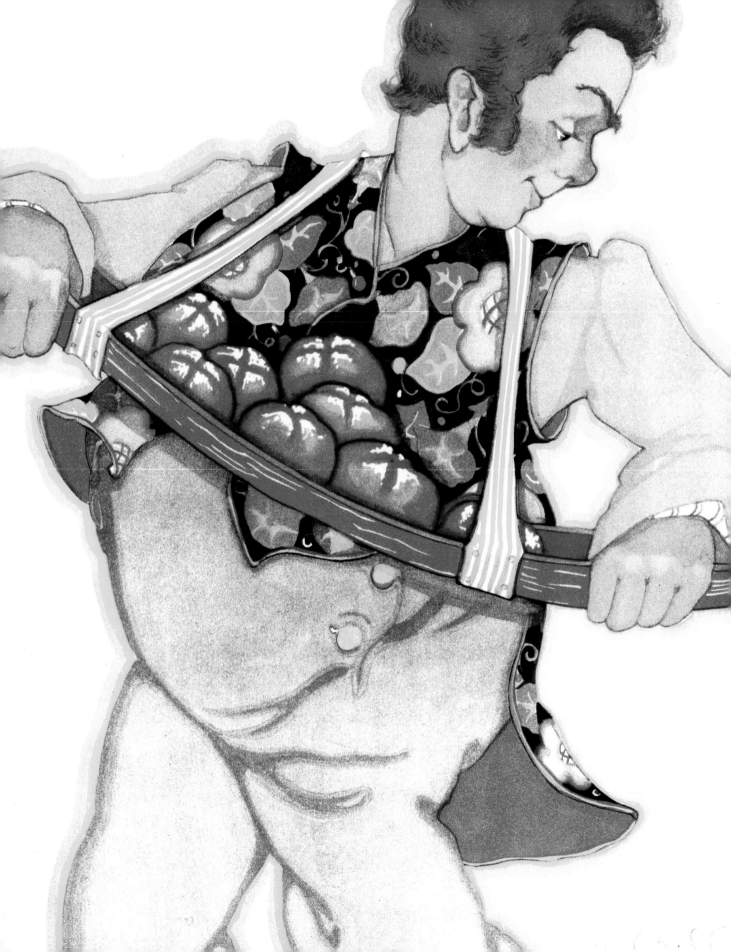

HOT CROSS BUNS

Hot cross buns!
Hot cross buns!
One a penny, two a penny,
Hot cross buns!

Hot cross buns!
Hot cross buns!
If you have no daughters,
Give them to your sons.

ROCK-A-BY, BABY

Rock-a-by, baby, rock,
   rock, rock,
Baby shall have a new
   pink frock!
A new pink frock, and a
   ribbon to tie,
If baby is good and
   ceases to cry.

Rock-a-by, baby, rock,
   rock, rock,
Listen, who comes with a
   knock, knock, knock?
Oh, it is pussy! Come in,
   come!
Mother and baby are
   always at home.

COCK-A-DOODLE-DOO

Cock-a-doodle-doo!
My dame has lost her shoe;
My master has lost his
   fiddling-stick,
And doesn't know what to do.

Cock-a-doodle-doo!
What is my dame to do?
Till master finds his
   fiddling-stick
She'll dance without her shoe.

135

DEEDLE, DEEDLE, DUMPLING

Deedle, deedle, dumpling, my son John,
He went to bed with his stockings on;
One shoe off, and one shoe on,
Deedle, deedle, dumpling, my son John.

CROSS PATCH

Cross Patch, draw the latch,
Sit by the fire and spin;
Take a cup, and drink it up,
Then call your neighbors in.

COME OUT TO PLAY

Girls and boys, come out
    to play,
The moon doth shine as
    bright as day;
Leave your supper, and
    leave your sleep,
And come with your
    playfellows into the
    street.

Come with a whoop,
    come with a call,
Come with a good will or
    not at all.
Up the ladder and down
    the wall,
A halfpenny roll will
    serve us all.
You find milk, and I'll
    find flour,
And we'll have pudding
    in half an hour.

CRY, BABY, CRY

Cry, baby, cry,
Put your fingers in
    your eye,
And tell your mother
    it wasn't I.

HOW DO YOU DO, NEIGHBOR

How do you do, neighbor?
Neighbor, how do you do?
Very well, I thank you,
How does Cousin Sue do?

She is very well,
And sends her love unto you,
And so does Cousin Bell.
Ah! how, pray, does she do?

THERE WAS A JOLLY MILLER

There was a jolly miller
Lived on the River Dee;
He worked and sang from morn till night,
No lark so blithe as he.
And this the burden of his song
For ever used to be—
I care for nobody—no! not I!
Since nobody cares for me.

OLD CHAIRS TO MEND

If I'd as much money
    as I could spend,
I never would cry old
    chairs to mend;
Old chairs to mend,
    old chairs to mend;
I never would cry old
    chairs to mend.

If I'd as much money
    as I could tell,
I never would cry old
    clothes to sell;
Old clothes to sell, old
    clothes to sell;
I never would cry old
    clothes to sell.

The Tale of Peter Rabbit

ONCE upon a time there were four little rabbits. Their names were:

> Flopsy,
>> Mopsy,
>>> Cotton-tail,
>>>> and Peter.

They lived with their mother in a sand bank. It was under the roots of a very big fir tree.

One morning Mrs. Rabbit said, "My dears, you may go into the fields. You may go down the lane. But don't go into Mr. McGregor's garden. Your father had an accident there. He was put into a pie by Mrs. McGregor.

"Now run along," said Mrs. Rabbit. "Don't get into mischief. I am going away." Mrs. Rabbit took a basket and her umbrella. She went through the woods to the market. Flopsy, Mopsy, and Cotton-tail were good little bunnies. They went down the lane to pick blackberries.

But Peter was very naughty. He ran right over to Mr. McGregor's garden, and squeezed under the gate. Peter ate some lettuce. He ate some beans. He ate some radishes. And then feeling sick he went to look for some parsley.

But at the end of the path whom should he see but Mr. McGregor. Mr. McGregor was working in the garden. He was setting out cabbages.

When he saw Peter he jumped up and ran after him. He waved his rake and called out, "Stop thief! Stop thief!"

Peter was very much frightened. He ran here. He ran there. He ran all over the garden. He could not find his way back to the gate.

He lost one shoe in the cabbage patch. He lost the other shoe in the potato patch. After that he ran on four legs. He could go faster then.

Peter could have got away if he had not run into a net. The large buttons on his jacket got caught in the net. It was a blue jacket with yellow buttons. It was very new.

Peter could not get away. He cried and cried. Some little sparrows heard him crying. They flew down to him. "Try, Peter! Try again!" they called.

Mr. McGregor heard the noise. He came running with a sieve to catch Peter.

Peter wiggled out just in time. But he left his new blue jacket with the yellow buttons behind him.

Peter ran into a shed. He jumped into a watering can. It would have been a good place to hide but the can had water in it. Mr. McGregor was sure that Peter was in the shed. He looked under all the flower pots. He looked everywhere. At last Peter sneezed, "Kerchoo! Kerchoo!"

Mr. McGregor was right after him. He tried to put his foot upon Peter. But Peter jumped out of a window. He upset three plants. Mr. McGregor was tired of running after Peter. He went back to his work.

Peter sat down to rest. He was very tired and frightened. He was very wet from sitting in the can.

After a while he began to look around. He found a door in a wall, but it was locked. There was no room for a fat little rabbit to squeeze under it.

An old mouse came by. She was carrying peas and beans to her family in the wood. Peter asked her the way to the gate. She had such a large pea in her mouth that she could not answer. She only shook her head at him.

Peter started to find his way across the garden. He came to the pond where Mr. McGregor filled his watering cans. A white cat was sitting by the pond. She was looking at some gold fish.

She sat very, very still. Now and then the tip of her tail moved as if it were alive. Peter thought it best not to talk to the cat. He had heard about cats from his cousin, Little Benjamin Bunny. He hopped on.

All at once he heard, "Scritch, scratch, scritch, scratch." It was the noise of a hoe.

Peter ran into the bushes. But when nothing happened he came out again. He climbed upon a wheelbarrow and peeped over.

The first thing he saw was Mr. McGregor. He was hoeing onions. He had his back to Peter. On the other side of him was a gate.

Peter got down off the wheelbarrow. He started running as fast as he could go. He ran along the path behind some bushes. Mr. McGregor saw him at the corner and started after him. But Peter did not care. He squeezed under the gate, and was safe at last in the wood outside the garden.

Mr. MacGregor hung up the little jacket and shoes for a scare-crow to frighten the black birds.

Peter never stopped running. He never looked behind him until he got home to the big fir tree. He was so tired! He flopped down upon the nice soft sand of the rabbit hole. He shut his eyes.

His mother was busy cooking. She looked at Peter. "What has he done with his clothes?" she said to herself. He has lost two jackets and two pairs of shoes in two weeks.

I am sorry to say that Peter was not very well that evening. His mother put him to bed. She made some camomile tea. She gave a dose of it to Peter. "One table-spoonful to be taken at bed-time."

Flopsy,

Mopsy,

and Cotton-tail

had bread and milk and blackber-ries with cream for supper.

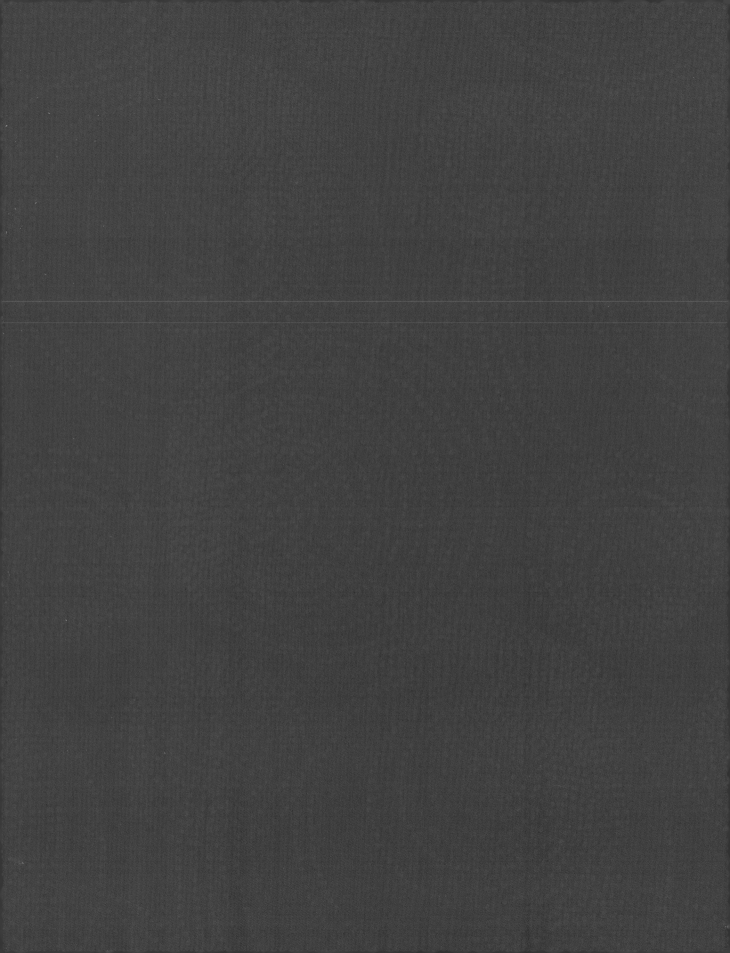

Cinderella

ONCE upon a time there lived a little girl who was very unhappy. She was sad because her mother had passed away. She lived with a cruel step-mother and two step-sisters. Her father lived with them too, but she hardly ever saw him.

The little girl had not always been unhappy. When her mother was living they used to play in the garden and laugh and sing all day. Her mother was beautiful and little Ella loved her very much.

But now she had no one to play with her. The step-sisters made her scrub and work very hard. They never called her by the name her mother had given her, but they called her "Cinderella." They made her sit in the kitchen when she was not waiting on them. They would say,

"Cinderella, bring me my purple dress," or

"Cinderella, where is my green petticoat I told you to wash?"

All day long Cinderella had to cook and run errands until she was so tired that at night she cried herself to sleep.

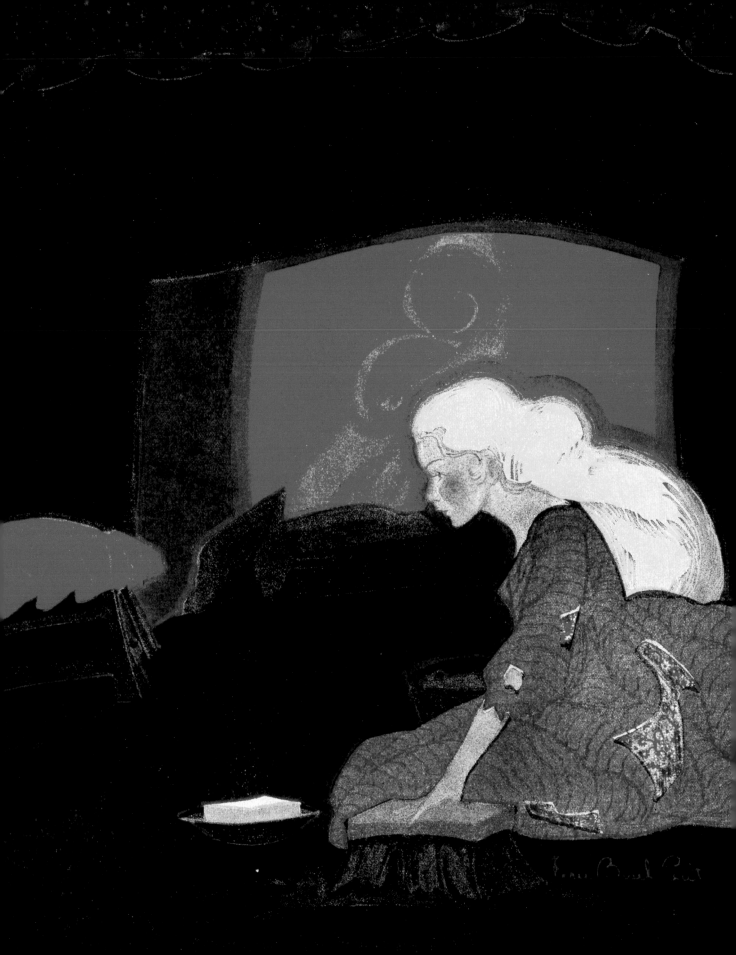

Now the step-mother and the two step-sisters were as ugly to look at as they were to live with. The step-mother was very short and very fat and had a hooked nose. Euphronia, the older sister, had red hair, a great big nose and such crossed-eyes that when one eye looked at Cinderella the other eye looked out of the window. Charlotte, the other sister, was not quite so ugly, but she was tall and thin and she had a very long nose. They were very cross to each other and to the servants. Indeed they were never nice to any one and so no one liked them.

Now in a town not far away lived the King and Queen and their only son. The son was soon to be twenty-one years old. On his birthday they were going to have many festivities. In the afternoon there was to be a party for all the children of the town. Every girl was to be given a doll and every boy a toy. And in the evening there was to be a beautiful ball.

"We shall be invited, for we are very important people," said Euphronia.

The next day the King's messenger rode up to the house with a large letter in his hand. It was an invitation to the ball!

"I shall wear my red dress with the yellow trimmings," said Euphronia.

"And I shall wear my black dress with blue ribbons," said Charlotte.

Poor Cinderella said nothing for she had only rags to wear. She knew she could not go to the ball in rags.

The great day came. Right after breakfast they began to dress for the ball, and oh, how Cinderella had to work!

"Cinderella, you must brush my hair until it looks like spun silk," said Charlotte.

"No, Charlotte, Cinderella must polish my shoe buckles and make them shine like stars," said Euphronia.

And while Cinderella ran hither and thither how she did wish she could go to the ball!

At last, night came and the ugly step-mother and sisters drove off in their dresses of silk and velvet. Cinderella sat down by the fire and cried and cried.

Suddenly she heard a little noise and there before her stood a little old woman. She was dressed in a purple petticoat, a blue cloak, and a funny tall, pointed hat.

"Why do you cry, little one?" said the old woman, smiling. When Cinderella saw the woman smile she was not in the least afraid of her.

Now Cinderella was ashamed of her tears, but she had to be polite, so she answered,

"I'm crying because I can't go to the ball, and see the Prince and all the beautiful things."

"Oh, but you can go to the ball!" said her godmother. "Run out into the garden and bring me the largest pumpkin you can find."

And when Cinderella brought the largest pumpkin from the garden her godmother said,

"Put it here by the door." And as Cinderella put it by the door her god-mother touched it with a funny little stick which she had in her hand. At once the pumpkin changed into a golden coach. It was all shining glass above and lined with blue satin.

"Now, Cinderella, go and see if there are any mice in the trap."

Cinderella ran and brought the trap with six mice in it.

"Now hold the door open and let them out one at a time."

And as Cinderella did so her godmother tapped each mouse with her wand and each mouse turned into a prancing gray horse with a long tail.

The horses were so well trained that they ran and took their places in front of the coach.

"Now, Cinderella, bring me the rat trap."

And there in the trap was a big fat rat with long whiskers. With a touch of the fairy's wand he was changed into a fine fat coachman. He took his place on the coach as if he had always been there.

"There, Cinderella, you can go to the ball," said her godmother, "and no one will look finer than you."

"Oh, but what shall I do for a dress? I can't go in these rags I have on!" cried Cinderella.

"Bless my soul! I forgot all about your dress. But we can fix that in no time," and her godmother touched Cinderella with her queer little stick. There stood Cinderella, not in her rags, but in a most beautiful dress of pink silk all embroidered with bees and butterflies. On her hair was a pearl pin. On her feet were pretty little glass slippers.

"There, Cinderella, you are all ready to drive off to the ball. Now have a good time, but you must remember this one thing! You must leave when the clock strikes twelve, for at that time your coach will become a pumpkin; your horses will become mice; your coachman

will become a rat; and you will have only your old ragged dress on. Remember!" And with these words the little old woman disappeared as quickly as she had come.

Oh what excitement there was when Cinderella was seen at the ball!

Everybody wondered who she might be. Her step-sisters did not know her and bowed very low before her. They thought she must be a princess at least. The Prince fell in love with her at first sight. He danced every dance with her.

But just before midnight Cinderella remembered what her godmother had said. So she said good night and thanked the King and Queen for the nice time she had had. The Prince did not want to let her go, but he was polite and when he saw she really wanted to go, he did not beg her to stay.

Just as the coach drove into the gate at home, the clock began to strike twelve. At the last stroke the beautiful coach disappeared; the prancing horses disappeared; the fat coachman disappeared. Only an old wrinkled pumpkin was left—and Cinderella saw the tails of the six gray mice and the fat gray rat disappear down the hole by the front door.

When her step-mother and sisters arrived a little later, Cinderella pretended to be so sleepy! They talked and talked of the beautiful lady who had appeared at the ball.

"She spoke to me so politely! Now how did she know my name?" said Charlotte.

"Oh, she wasn't nearly so nice to you as she was to me!" said Euphronia. Euphronia was as cross as usual, for no one had danced with her all the evening, and only the strange Princess had spoken to her at all.

The next evening the same thing happened. No sooner had the step-mother and sisters driven off to the palace than the little old woman appeared.

Soon Cinderella's coach with its six horses and sleek fat coachman stood ready at the door. This time, however, Cinderella's dress was prettier than ever. It was all yellow satin. Around her neck was a neck-lace of pearls, and on her feet were the same glass slippers, painted with gold butterflies.

When she arrived at the palace the Prince was waiting impatiently, looking this way and that for her. He was so afraid the beautiful strange lady would not come.

"At last, I see her!" he cried, and he led Cinderella into the ball room. Again all evening he would not leave her side. He danced every dance with her, and looked at no one else. Cinderella had such a good time that she forgot all about what her godmother had said. It was only when the clock began to strike twelve that she remembered. She did not wait to

say good night but ran down the steps of the palace. She ran so fast that she dropped one of her glass slippers and just as she got to the palace garden she heard the last stroke of twelve. Her beautiful yellow dress disappeared and she had on only her old rags. Oh, how ashamed she was! She crept through the palace gates. The guards were surprised to see a little kitchen maid at that time of night.

The King sent word that every woman in his kingdom must try on the glass slipper which was lost by the beautiful lady. All day his men went from house to house. At last they came to Cinderella's home.

The ugly step-mother took the slipper first but she could not make it go on her foot. Then Euphronia tried, but she could not make the slipper go on. Charlotte was the next to try. She grunted and groaned as she tried to get it on, but the slipper would not even go over her great toe!

"Is there no other lady in the house?" politely asked the messenger.

"There is only our kitchen maid, but of course that ugly thing could not wear the slipper," said Euphronia.

"But His Majesty, the King, said every woman must try on the slipper," said the messenger.

Then Cinderella came forward and of course her foot slipped into the glass slipper, for had it not been made for her? When the messenger

saw this he bowed low before her.

Suddenly the old godmother appeared and once more Cinderella was dressed as she had been dressed the night before. The coach stood at the door, and when Cinderella drove up to the palace there was no one happier than the Prince to see his beautiful lady again. They were married the very next day.

Now, although the step-mother and sisters had been so cruel to her, Cinderella was kind to them. She had them come to live at the palace. There they all lived happily ever after. They lived so happily that even the sisters grew to be kind, and every one loved them almost as much as they loved Cinderella!

Purr and Miew Kitten Stories

THE ACCIDENT AT THE POND

MRS. PURR-MIEW was proud of her family. She was proud of her three fluffy kittens, Hop, Skip, and Jump, and she was proud of her big, handsome husband.

She was proud also of her husband's ancestry. His Great-grandfather Purr-Miew had been born in Persia and had lived in the royal palace most of his life. Later he had come to America. Many tales of his life in the palace had he told Thomas Purr-Miew when Thomas was a little kitten; tales of how he had fished for goldfish in the fountain under the palms in the courtyard, how he had been fed sugar plums by all the lovely ladies of the court, and how he had enjoyed the tasty mice he had caught in the pantries of the palace.

Besides being proud of her kittens and her husband, Mother Purr-Miew was also proud of her house. It was a charming little gray shingle house with a real knocker on the door. Five years ago the Carpenter Cat had built it in the middle of the yard under a pear tree. Father Purr-Miew had planted a catnip hedge around it. When the house was finished, Mr. Maltese had papered the rooms for them. He had chosen one paper in a striped pattern, one in a plaid, and another in a bird-fish-mouse-milk design which Hop, Skip, and Jump liked very much. In his Great-grandfather's trunk, Father Purr-Miew had found a famous painting, "Mouse Trap and Cheese," by Sir Angora. This they had hung on the living-room wall.

Early on the day on which this story begins, Mother Purr-Miew had been busy baking bread and cookies. Little Jump, who had been taking a nap, awoke about three o'clock and went outside to find Hop and Skip. A few minutes later she came into the house with tears in her eyes.

"Mother," said she, "Hop and Skip have gone away without taking me."

"Never mind, dear," replied Mother, wiping Jump's teary eyes with her apron. "They have gone down to the pond to slide. If you like, you may go too."

With her tears quite forgotten, little Jump ran out of the house and across the fields toward the pond, and Mother Purr-Miew returned to her baking.

But now Mother Purr-Miew was troubled. It was five o'clock and Hop, Skip, and Jump had not come home. She looked out of the window across the snowy fields, but not one kitten could she see.

"Where can they be?" said she with a sigh. "I do hope they haven't met with an accident. I know," she went on. "I will wake up Father Purr-Miew and ask him to look for them."

So Mother Purr-Miew went up the little stairs and into the room where Father Purr-Miew was sleeping soundly after a hard night's work catching mice and rats in the farmer's barn.

"Thomas!" said Mother Purr-Miew, "wake up; it is five o'clock and the kittens are not home yet. I have supper all ready."

"I shall get dressed and go to look for them at once," answered Father Purr-Miew. "It is time for me to get up anyway."

So Father Purr-Miew put on his clothes and, wrapping his warmest muffler around his neck, went out of the house and off across the fields.

Though it was snowing quite hard, he could still see traces of the kittens' footprints in the snow, and he followed them toward the pond.

He felt so anxious that he began to run. Down the hill and across the field he sped. At last he reached the bank of the pond and then he saw the kittens. They had broken through the ice, and he could see their little heads bobbing around in the water like three corks.

"Why, you poor little kittens!" cried Father Purr-Miew. "I will have you out of there in a jiffy."

With this he ran to the fence. After a little search he found a loose board. Dragging the board to the edge of the ice, he pushed it out on to the face of the pond so that it rested across the hole. Then, stepping gingerly, he crept out upon the board until he could reach the kittens. Lifting them out one at a time, he carried them safely to shore.

Such bedraggled little kittens you never saw. Their fur and clothes were dripping water, Hop had lost his cap, and all three had lost their mittens.

"Now," said Father Purr-Miew, "we shall run as fast as we can to the house, and the faster we run, the warmer you will be."

Back up the hill and across the fields they ran, but despite the speed at which they went, they were a distressing sight before they reached the house, for their fur and clothes were covered with icicles.

Mother was waiting for them at the door, and she said, "You funny looking little kittens! You must have had an accident."

"We fell in the pond," said Hop.

"The ice broke!" said Skip.

"And we lost our mittens," added Jump.

"You poor little kittens!" said Mother anxiously. "Father and I will help you take off your clothes and get you into a hot bath. That will melt the icicles and keep you from catching cold."

Soon the kittens were dressed in dry clothes, and they came downstairs to the supper table where Mother Purr-Miew had some nice hot milk waiting for them. While they drank their milk they told their father and mother of their afternoon's adventures.

"Well," said Mother Purr-Miew, "it is a mercy that you all were able to swim."

"Yes," agreed Father Purr-Miew, "and it's a good thing that little kittens are supposed to have nine lives!"

Then Father Purr-Miew lighted his lantern and, saying good-night to Mother Purr-Miew and the three little kittens, went out of the house on his way to the barn to do his night's work.

THE CARPENTER CAT

ALL through the night the snow fell in great fleecy flakes. It piled in deep drifts against the fences; it left blankets on the housetops and tall white caps on the chimneys.

The next morning, after the kittens had had their breakfast, Hop asked, "Mother, may we go out to play in the snow?"

"Yes, you may," Mother Purr-Miew replied, "but you will have to wear your new Christmas mittens, since you lost your old ones in the pond."

The kittens purred with delight. They ran to find their mittens and were soon outside having a wonderful time in the deep drifts. Their mittens were so clean and new that they took them off for fear of getting them wet. At that moment the Carpenter Cat came chugging up the road in his funny automobile. As he passed the house, the kittens held up their mittens and called to him, "Look, Mr. Carpenter Cat, see the new mittens that we got for Christmas?"

"Yes indeed," the Carpenter Cat replied, stopping his automobile. "They are pretty mittens, too." Then he added, "Ask your mother if you may go with me to the new house I am building."

Mother Purr-Miew gave her consent at once, knowing the Carpenter Cat to be a very responsible fellow and quite fond of the kittens, and soon they were on their way up the road.

When they reached the new house the Carpenter Cat said, "Now Hop, Skip, and Jump, you must be very careful not to go near the holes in the floor. You can have all these curly shavings to play with."

For a time the kittens played with the shavings. Then tiring of this, they sat down on a pile of lumber and watched the Carpenter Cat as he planed a long board until it was perfectly smooth.

"Kittens, have you a sled?" asked the Carpenter Cat at last.

"No, Mr. Carpenter Cat, we haven't," they replied.

"Well, little kittens should have a sled," said he. "How would you like to have me make one for you?"

The kittens were so overjoyed at the idea that Hop gave a little hop, Skip gave a little skip, and Jump gave a little jump.

So the Carpenter Cat measured off two pieces of board and shaped them for the runners and cut some smaller pieces for the braces and a wide piece for the top. As he worked he said, "I wish I knew how to put some magic in your sled so it would be an up-hill sled."

"What is an up-hill sled, Mr. Carpenter Cat?" asked Hop.

"An up-hill sled is one that will coast up hill instead of down," the Carpenter Cat replied. "I heard of a sled like that once that belonged to a little boy who was too lazy to pull his sled up the coasting hill. The story goes like this:"

Lazy little Johnny Tubbs sat on his sled at the foot of the long coasting hill and grumbled and grumbled.

"I wish my sled was an up-hill sled," said he; "I wish that it would go up hill as easily as it comes down."

"Ho, ho, ho!" a creaky little voice piped up.

Johnny looked around and saw a tiny snow-elf sitting cross-legged in a snowdrift.

"Well, it's no laughing matter!" said Johnny crossly.

"Ho! It's no grumbling matter!" answered the snow-elf, straightening

up suddenly. "If you want an up-hill sled, all you have to say is the magic word 'Upsy-sledsy!' Just lie down on your sled, take a good hold, then say 'Upsy-sledsy' and see what happens."

Johnny did as the snow-elf bade him, and the result was so unexpected and startling that Johnny slid off in to the snow as his sled went whisking up the coasting hill at a terrific speed.

Johnny jumped up and ran after it. He reached the hilltop very much out of breath and was delighted to find his sled lying in the snow at the top of the slide looking quite as if nothing had happened.

He picked it up, took a running start, and threw himself on it, expecting to go scooting down the hill just as he had always done. But he met with a sudden and painful surprise. For, although the hill was as smooth as glass, Johnny's sled stopped with a suddenness that sent him flying over the head of it, bumping his little nose so hard on the packed snow that the tears came to his eyes.

"Ho, ho!" laughed the little snow-elf, appearing at the top of the hill right at this instant. "I forgot to tell you that an up-hill sled has to be carried down hill. But then you should not mind that very much, for it's a lot easier to walk down hill with your sled than it is to walk up with one."

"Yes, I guess that's right!" answered Johnny.

"Now before I leave you, Johnny," said the snow-elf, "there is one thing I must tell you. Never, never say 'Upsy-downsy' to your sled, for that's another magic word, and I don't want to be responsible for the consequences."

With this the snow-elf disappeared in a big snowdrift. But all that day Johnny had heaps of fun sliding up hill on his up-hill sled, and for awhile at least he did not seem to care that he had to carry it down.

"But did Johnny ever say the magic word 'Upsy-downsy' to his sled?" asked Hop.

"Did he?" echoed Skip.

"Yes, did he?" lisped Jump.

"Well, that's another story," the Carpenter Cat replied, picking up his tools and putting them away in his tool box. "I shall have to wait until some other time to tell you about that for it's twelve o'clock and time for little kittens and Carpenter Cats to have their lunch. So I will take you home now, but if your mother says that it will be all right, I will stop for you after lunch and bring you back. Then I can tell you what happened when little Johnny said 'Upsy-downsy' to his sled."

With this the Carpenter Cat helped the kittens into the automobile and soon they were on their way down the snowy road toward the Purr-Miew house.

WHAT HAPPENED TO THE UP-HILL SLED

THE clock on the kitchen shelf was just striking twelve when Mother Purr-Miew went to the window and looked expectantly up the road.

"I think since the Carpenter Cat has been so kind that it would be nice to invite him to stop and have lunch with us." She looked up the

road but saw no signs of the Carpenter Cat's automobile. "Well," said she, turning away from the window, "they will be along very soon, for the Carpenter Cat always passes the house around noontime."

She went to the oven and opened it and took out a cherry pie which she had been baking for lunch.

"I do hope the Carpenter Cat likes cherry pie," said she as she put the pie on the table.

The big hand on the kitchen clock moved slowly around until it pointed to fifteen minutes after twelve. Immediately Mother Purr-Miew heard a loud chug-chugging out in the road, and the Carpenter Cat's automobile stopped in front of the house.

"Mr. Carpenter Cat," called Mother from the doorway, "won't you come in and have lunch with us this noon? I have made a cherry pie. Do you like cherry pie?"

"Thank you, I shall be glad to have lunch with you, and I do like cherry pie," said the Carpenter Cat, answering both questions at once.

The kittens were delighted at the thought of the Carpenter Cat having lunch with them, and they made a gay procession as they all went up the walk to the house.

"Hop, please go upstairs and awaken Father. Tell him that lunch is ready," said Mother Purr-Miew. Hop ran up the stairs and came down very soon, followed by his father.

"How do you do, Mr. Carpenter Cat?" said Father Purr-Miew. "How are you this fine wintry day?"

"I am quite well, thank you, Mr. Purr-Miew," the Carpenter Cat replied. They all gathered around the table and when they were seated, the Carpenter Cat said, "How is the Mousing and Ratting Business, Mr. Purr-Miew?"

"Brisk, Mr. Carpenter Cat, very brisk," Father Purr-Miew replied. "I caught five rats last night. I take my pay in fresh milk and cream, and the more rats and mice I catch, the more milk and cream I get."

After every smidge of the cherry pie had been eaten and Hop, Skip, and Jump had drunk their milk, the Carpenter Cat took the three kittens aboard his automobile and they went back to the new house.

"Now," said the Carpenter Cat after they had arrived, "I shall give your sled a coat of red paint." With this he opened a little shed beside the house and took out a can of paint. Prying off the lid, he began to stir the paint with a stick.

"Now will you tell us what happened to Johnny when he said 'Upsy-downsy' to his sled?" asked Hop.

"I'll do just that," said the Carpenter Cat. "Come over here so you can sit near me."

The kittens obeyed and the Carpenter Cat went on with the story:

"Isn't it fun to coast on an up-hill sled, Johnny?" said the little snow-elf, hopping up and down in a snowdrift and laughing in his creaky little voice.

"No, it isn't! The other boys don't like my sled," he replied crossly. "They say we'll bump into one another if I coast up hill when they are coasting down, so they have made me find another coasting hill."

"Ho, ho!" laughed the snow-elf. "I hope you aren't tired of your up-hill sled so soon."

"No, I'm not tired of it," answered Johnny. "It's much easier to walk down hill than up, but I wish it was an up-hill and a down-hill sled too. Then I wouldn't have to walk at all."

"Oh, no, you don't, Johnny," said the elf. "That would never, never do at all. You are too lazy now. If you had a sled that coasted both ways, it would be sure to bring you trouble. And remember, Johnny, never say 'Upsy-downsy' to your sled." With this the snow-elf went swirling away in a gust of wind like a snowflake.

"I wonder why he doesn't want me to say 'Upsy-downsy,'" thought Johnny after the elf had disappeared. "I bet it's because that would make the sled coast both ways."

The more Johnny thought about it, the more convinced he became that these were the magic words which would make his sled do everything he would like it to do. So at last he plumped himself down on the sled and said, "Upsy-downsy."

No sooner were the words out of his mouth than the sled raced off across the fields, up hill and down hill, bounding, bumping over hummocks and gulleys, jumping fences, skimming across ponds, until Johnny was quite out of breath.

As the sled rushed along, it came to a barnyard, and a big haystack was right in its path. Johnny's hair stood straight up as he saw the haystack draw nearer and nearer. To add to his terror, he found that he could not let go of the sled. Then just as he shut his eyes and prepared for a bump, the sled coasted up one side of the stack and down the other so quickly and smoothly that Johnny barely knew it had happened.

On went the sled across the barnyard and headed for a big red barn. "Surely it can never go over that!" thought Johnny, but before he could say "Jack Robinson," the surprising sled shot right up one side of the

barn, over the roof tree, and down on the other side. Over the barnyard gate it went and out on to the road to town.

Then began the most thrilling ride that had ever been seen on the highway. There were many folks on their way to market that day, and as the magic sled went skimming by, it left a long trail of frightened, rearing horses, upset wagons, topsy-turvy boxes and crates, squawking chickens, broken eggs, and bruised vegetables.

When the sled reached the outskirts of the town, instead of coasting down the wide Main Street, it carried Johnny right up the side of the first house and began some antics over the roofs of the houses. The houses were all quite close together and their steep roofs made a row of perfect coasting hills over which Johnny's sled raced, up and down, up and down, like a roller coaster. To add to the excitement, the street was full of folks all waving their arms and talking at once, with some running along beside the houses in a vain endeavor to keep up with the sled.

When the sled reached the last rooftop, it fell into a chimney and down it went into the black depths, leaving Johnny so tightly wedged in the chimney mouth that it took the town fire department a half hour to get him out.

"But what became of Johnny's sled?" asked Hop. "Was it all burned up?"

"Some say it was," answered the Carpenter Cat, "and some say that it coasted right out of the fireplace and out of the house into the street, and that it is coasting yet."

"I'm glad our sled isn't an Upsy-downsy sled," said Hop.

"So am I," added Skip.

"Me too," echoed Jump.

MOTHER PURR-MIEW'S BIRTHDAY

M OTHER," said Hop one day, running into the kitchen where Mother Purr-Miew was working, "tomorrow is your birthday, isn't it?"

"Yes, it is," his mother answered.

"Oh, Mother, and we haven't any pennies to buy you a present!" said Hop. "Jump took the pennies out of the toy bank, and when she was playing soldier with them on the doorstep, they rolled into a crack and we couldn't find them any more."

"Never mind, Hop," said Mother consolingly. "There are other things that are just as nice as presents you buy in a store. Why don't you play you are three Good Fairies, and tomorrow you can help me with the housework."

"Oh, I know something better than that," said Hop eagerly. "We'll be three Good Fairies and do all the housework, and you can sit down in your easy chair and have a nice rest all day."

"We'll clean up the house and get all the meals," said Skip.

"And we'll bake you a birthday cake and put candles on it," lisped Jump.

The next morning when Mother Purr-Miew woke up, she heard some little feet pattering up the stairs, and into her room came a little procession. It was Hop, Skip, and Jump, with Hop in the lead carrying a tray on which was a bowl of oatmeal, two pieces of toast, and a glass of milk.

"Happy birthday, Mother!" the kittens cried. "We've brought your breakfast."

"Breakfast in bed?" said their mother. "How nice! It's been a long time since I have had breakfast in bed."

"It's just like being sick, isn't it, Mother?" said Jump.

After breakfast, Mother Purr-Miew dressed and came downstairs. The kittens put her in the easy chair with the flowers on it, and told her she did not have to move until she wished. They washed and wiped the breakfast dishes, then ran upstairs to make the beds. They picked up their little nighties and hung them in the closet, then they made their own little beds—and a good job they did too. All but Jump, who could not quite get the lumps and wrinkles out of hers.

When this was done, Hop gave Jump a ride on the carpet sweeper as he brushed up the carpets. While Hop ran the carpet sweeper, Skip dusted the furniture. The birds, the fish, the mice, and the milk bottles must have been surprised as they looked down from their places on the wall paper and watched these speedy little Fairies, for never had they seen Mrs. Purr-Miew whisk around as did these little kittens, hopping, skipping, and jumping from one room to another, and sliding down the banisters instead of using the stairs.

After lunch, which the kittens had prepared with no mishap, Hop said, "Now we must pitch in and make Mother's birthday cake."

They all went to the kitchen and there was a great deal of whispering in the corner by the stove as to just which was the right method of making a birthday cake.

"I know you use flour," offered Skip.

"And candles," added Jump. "Don't forget the candles, Skip."

"Yes, but how much flour?" asked Hop.

The little kittens rubbed their heads thoughtfully. Then Hop said, "I don't think it will spoil Mother's birthday if we ask her, do you?"

"Mother," he called through the kitchen door, "When Good Fairies are making a birthday cake for someone, how much flour do they use?"

Mother laughed and answered, "If I were a Good Fairy and were making a birthday cake for someone, I should pull a chair up beside the cupboard and take down the blue cook book from the top shelf, and then I should look on the page that says CAKES until I found a recipe for the kind of cake that I wanted to make. When I found it, I should read it and follow the instructions very carefully."

So Hop pulled a chair up beside the cupboard and took down the blue cook book. Opening it out on the floor, the three little kittens lay down on their stomachs around it, and Hop turned the pages until they came to the word CAKES. Picking out a recipe for SPONGE CAKE, he read the instructions to Skip and Jump.

"I think that will do very nicely," said Skip. "It hasn't any frosting, but frosting is very hard to make."

"Mother won't care if it doesn't have frosting if it has candles on it," said Jump.

"Let's start right away," said Hop. "Skip, you get out the blue bowl while I get the pan. Jump, you open the flour bin and bring me a sifter full of flour."

Jump ran to do Hop's bidding, and then occurred the first mishap of the day. For as the eager little kitten leaned over the edge of the flourbin, she fell in, and when Hop and Skip lifted her out, lo and behold, she had changed into a snow-white kitten.

Hop and Skip dusted Jump off with the broom, and then they all went back to the cake baking. After many a reading of the recipe and a great deal of effort in the mixing, the cake was at last in the pan and ready for the oven.

"How do you tell when the cake is done?" asked Hop after much peering into the oven.

"Oh, I know," answered Skip. "Mother pokes straws into it." So what did Hop do but stick a handful of broom straws into the cake so that it looked like a young porcupine.

"Oh, not that way!" said Skip, coming to the rescue. "She sticks only one straw in the cake and then she pulls it right out again. And if the straw isn't sticky, why, the cake is done."

"Well," said Hop skeptically, "I think we'd better have Mother look at it, then we will be sure that it is done."

That night when they were all around the supper table, Mother Purr-Miew said to her husband, "Thomas, I have had such a restful day. There were three Good Fairies in the house and they did all the work."

"I'm sorry that I was not awake to see them," said Thomas Purr-Miew, "for I have never seen a Good Fairy."

When they were all ready for their dessert, the kittens went to the kitchen, and Hop lighted the candles on the cake. Then with Jump in the lead proudly bearing the candle-lit cake, the three kittens marched back into the dining-room.

"You must make a wish before you blow out the candles, Mother," said Hop.

So Mother made a wish and then she blew out the candles with one big puff.

BOBBY WILD-CAT

LOOK, Mother, our mittens are dry," said Hop after lunch as the three little kittens came into the dining-room.

"Yes," said Mother Purr-Miew, "you may put them on and go outside."

"May we go down to the Big Woods to visit Bobby Wild-Cat?" asked Hop.

"You may if you like. But don't go too far or you might get lost," answered Mother Purr-Miew.

The kittens put on their mittens and started down the road toward the Big Woods. On the way they met Sammy and Mandy Black-Cat.

"Where are you all going?" asked Sammy.

"We're going down to the Big Woods to play with Bobby Wild-Cat. Do you want to come along?" said Hop.

"Yes, we'd like to," said Sammy and Mandy eagerly.

They all trailed down the road until they came to a rail fence. Climbing through the fence, the kittens found themselves in the Big Woods.

As they went along over a path carpeted with pine needles, they met little Petey Pup.

"Where are you going, kittens?" asked Petey Pup.

"We're going into the Big Woods to play with Bobby Wild-Cat. Do you want to come along?" said Hop.

"But you must promise not to chase us up trees," said little Jump.

"Oh, I'll promise not to chase you up trees," said Petey Pup. And he joined the merry procession through the woods.

They had not gone far when they met little Johnny Rabbit.

"Where are you going?" asked Johnny Rabbit.

"We're going into the Big Woods to play with Bobby Wild-Cat. Would you like to come along, Johnny Rabbit?" said Hop.

"Yes, I should like that," said Johnny Rabbit. "But I hope Petey Pup won't chase me into stumps."

Petey Pup promised that he would not chase him into stumps, and he joined the happy group, and they all went on their way. Presently they met little Reddy Fox slyly picking his way through the underbrush.

"Where are you going?" asked Reddy Fox.

"We're on our way into the Big Woods to play with Bobby Wild-Cat. Would you like to come along?" said Hop.

"I think that would be fun," said Reddy Fox.

"But don't you try to nibble me, Reddy Fox, or I shall go back home," said Johnny Rabbit.

"Oh, I won't nibble very hard," said Reddy Fox, who just couldn't resist nibbling little rabbits when he got a chance.

"Let's play we are a parade," said Hop.

"Let's be a band. I'll play the bass drum," said Skip.

"All right, you can play the bass drum, Skip, and the rest of you can play the horns. I will be the Drum Major," said Hop. Picking up a long stick, he began to twirl it around his head.

So they marched along the path with Hop walking very stiffly and twirling his stick, and Jump, Sammy, Mandy, Petey Pup, Johnny Rabbit, and Reddy Fox all making "oompah! oompah!" sounds like horns, while

Skip brought up the rear making a loud "boom! boom! boom!" like a bass drum.

At last they came to the little cave house where Bobby Wild-Cat lived. All marched up to the front door, and Hop knocked with his stick. Mrs. Wild-Cat opened the door and said, "Why, you sound just like a brass band."

"We are a brass band," said Hop. "Don't we play well?"

"I suppose you are looking for Bobby?" said Mrs. Wild-Cat.

"Yes," said Hop. "We want him to play with us."

"He could if he were here," said Mrs. Wild-Cat, "but he went over to Mr. Owl's house. If you like, you may go over there and find him. I know he will be glad to play with you. He is a very restless little kitten."

The merry little group filed out into the path again, and singing at the tops of their voices, they made their way toward Mr. Owl's house.

Mr. Owl lived in an old pine tree which was quite hollow inside. A rustic stairway led up to his front door, which was cut in the side of the tree.

The gay procession marched up the little stairway, and Hop rang the bell at the side of the door.

"How do you do, Mr. Owl?" said Hop politely, when Mr. Owl came to the door. "We are looking for Bobby Wild-Cat. Is he here?"

"Yes, he is," answered Mr. Owl. "Won't you come in? I have some candy mice for you."

The kittens, the pup, the rabbit, and the fox all entered Mr. Owl's house, and they found Bobby Wild-Cat sitting on the sofa nibbling at a candy mouse. Mr. Owl passed the candy mice around.

"Haven't you any candy rabbits?" inquired Reddy Fox. "I prefer them."

"I'd like a candy bone," said Petey Pup.

"And as for me," said Johnny Rabbit, "I should like some candy turnips."

"No," said Mr. Owl, "I have only candy mice. But if you try them, you will find them very nice."

So they all sat down. There were not enough chairs in Mr. Owl's little house for all of them, so some had to sit on the floor. But they did not mind that for the candy mice tasted very good.

They finished their sweets, and after thanking Mr. Owl, went outside to play. Bobby Wild-Cat went with them.

"I can snarl," said he proudly.

Hop, Skip, and Jump looked shocked, for their mother had often told them not to make snarling noises.

"Yes, and I can spit and scratch, too!" added the little wild-cat boastfully.

"We could too, if we wanted to," said Hop. "But Mother says it isn't polite."

"All wild-cats snarl and spit and scratch," said Bobby Wild-Cat stubbornly.

"But they can't bark! I can bark!" said Petey Pup, who was not to be outdone.

"So can I," said Reddy Fox.

"What shall we play?" said Johnny Rabbit, wishing to change the subject.

"Let's find a tall tree and see who can climb the highest," said Bobby Wild-Cat. "I dare you to climb to the top of this one," said he, running to a very tall, straight pine with but few limbs on it.

"You go first, Bobby," said Hop. "If you can do it, I can too." Bobby Wild-Cat ran up the tree, clutching the bark with his sharp claws. Up, up he went until he had reached the very top of it. When he came down he said, "There! I dare you to do it, Hop."

Hop was not to be dared, and he ran up the tree quite as fast as Bobby Wild-Cat had done. He ran to the very top, too; then he climbed down. Now Sammy, Mandy, and Skip each had a turn.

"May I climb it, too, Hop?" asked Jump.

"No, Jump, you are too small. Mother would not like to have you climb such a tall tree. Besides it is getting late and I think we should start home."

Bobby Wild-Cat, Johnny Rabbit, and Reddy Fox all went back with the kittens and the pup to the rail fence at the edge of the woods. It was just as Hop was preparing to climb through the fence that he discovered that Jump was not with the band.

"I hope she isn't lost," said Hop.

"We must go back and look for her," added Skip.

It was a worried little group that made their way back up the path for, search as they might, they saw no traces of the lost kitten. At last they reached the tall pine again. And as they came close to the foot of it, they heard a faint mewing, and there was Jump high up in the top and unable to get down.

As Bobby Wild-Cat was the biggest, he climbed up the tree, and taking Jump in his mouth, brought her safely to the ground.

"Anyway, I climbed the tree, even if I couldn't get down," said Jump as they all went back toward home.

THE KITTENS ARE LOST IN THE WOODS

ONE afternoon early in the month of May, the kittens went out into the Big Woods to look for wild flowers.

Although the sky was blue and cloudless and the sun was shining brightly, there was a chilly wind blowing, and so the kittens wore their coats and their Christmas mittens.

Farther and farther into the Big Woods the kittens wandered, forgetting that their mother had told them that they must not go far.

By the time the sun was dipping behind the trees, the three little kittens had each picked a bunch of flowers and then they turned to go home. As they trudged along through the thick underbrush, they became more and more confused, for they could not find the path which led to the edge of the woods. When they were beginning to feel quite discouraged, they met a little bear cub carrying a basket of dried berries.

"Hello, Kittens," said the cub. "What are you doing out here in the Big Woods?"

"We're lost!" said Hop with a woeful look. "Could you show us the way home?"

"Oh, I've never been outside the Big Woods," said the cub. "Mother doesn't allow me to go where I am liable to meet human folks who like to shoot little bears."

"Oh, dear, whatever shall we do?" said Hop.

"I'm so hungry," said Skip.

"And I'm so tired," said little Jump.

"You must come home with me and perhaps Mother can help you," said the cub.

The cub led the way through the underbrush, and as they all went along he said, "My name is Cubby Bear. What are your names?"

"Mine is Hop, and this is Skip, and this is Jump," Hop replied.

Presently they came to a cave in the side of a rocky hill. It had a window in it and a heavy wooden door.

"This is the cave house where I live," said Cubby. "Come in and see my mother."

Mrs. Bear greeted them kindly and listened to the kittens' troubles. "It is so late and you are so tired that perhaps you had better stay here all night. Then tomorrow I shall take you back to the edge of the woods. Come to the table; supper is ready," said she.

The thought of something to eat made the hungry kittens forget their homesickness, and they gladly found places at the table. But what was their disappointment when Mrs. Bear set before each a plate of wild roots and dried berries!

Hop and Skip were so polite that they did not say anything but bravely tried to nibble at their food. Not so Jump, however, for she piped up, "Haven't you any milk? I don't like roots and berries."

"No, I haven't," said Mrs. Bear, looking worried, "but tomorrow morning I shall go out and find some honey for your breakfast. Perhaps you would like that."

When the supper was over and the three little kittens were tucked into bed beside Cubby Bear, Mrs. Bear said, "Now I shall tell you a story about a little bear."

Once upon a time there was a little bear named Fuzzy who lived with his mother in a cave just like this. One day he had gone down to his Grandfather's house to take him a sack of acorns.

He gave his Grandfather the acorns and then he started home with the empty sack over his shoulder. On the way he saw a round prickly-looking object in the path.

"Well, of all things!" he exclaimed excitedly. "If it isn't a pin cushion full of needles! I shall take them home to Mother."

Reaching down, Fuzzy tried to pick up the object. But the moment he touched it, he squealed with pain and looked at his little paw. It was full of prickly needles. Then Fuzzy thought of a better way. He opened the empty acorn sack and with a stick he quickly poked the pin cushion in to the sack.

"There!" he cried gleefully. "Won't Mother be surprised when she sees what I have brought her?"

When Fuzzy got back to his cave house he put the sack on the table and told his mother to look inside and see the nice needles he had brought to her. But before Mother could touch the sack, it began to bounce around like a rubber ball, and the next thing they knew, it had gone *Plop!* right off the table onto the floor, and was flopping, hopping, and zigzagging around the cave in a very ridiculous manner.

"Land sakes alive!" exclaimed Mrs. Bear. "I never saw a sack act like that before! What in the world is in it?"

Making a quick lunge, Mrs. Bear caught hold of the sack. She opened it and she shook it out. And what do you suppose came out of it? A baby porcupine! And away that little porcupine went out of the door and down the path to find his mother.

Barely had Mother Bear finished this story when they all heard voices outside, and looking out of the window, they saw a number of lights bobbing along through the woods.

Nearer and nearer they came, right up to the door of the cave house. Mother Bear ran to open the door and into the cave crowded Father Purr-Miew, the Carpenter Cat, Pappy Black-Cat, Mr. Maltese, and the Constable Cat, all carrying lanterns.

They looked very much relieved when they saw the lost kittens safe and sound in Mrs. Bear's cave house.

After the kittens were dressed and Mrs. Bear had been thanked properly, Thomas Purr-Miew, carrying Jump on his shoulder, led the way out of the cave, and the searching party with the lost kittens made their way through the woods to an old Sawmill Road. There they found the Carpenter Cat's automobile waiting to take them home.

"Oh, you funny little kittens!" exclaimed Mother Purr-Miew, when Hop, Skip, and Jump were safely at home. "I am so glad to see you! Did you get lost in the woods?"

"Yes, we did," said Hop.

"And we had supper at Mrs. Bear's house," said Skip.

"We had to eat old roots and berries. I'm so hungry, Mother." added little Jump.

Mother Purr-Miew went to the kitchen and brought in the remains of a cherry pie which she had baked for supper. Cutting a piece for each, she put it on the table.

"There, you starved little kittens," said she, "help yourselves!"

Then what do you suppose those little kittens did? Why, they were all so hungry that they sat down and ate their pie without taking off their mittens.

Rumpelstiltzkin

ONCE upon a time there was a poor miller who wished the king to think him a great man. So one day he told the king that he had a beautiful daughter who could spin straw into gold.

"That is wonderful," said the king. "If your daughter is so clever, bring her to the palace, and I will put her to the test."

The miller took the girl to the palace the next day. The king led her to a room full of straw. Then he gave her a spinning wheel and a spindle and said to her, "Now set to work. If you have not spun all the straw into gold by dawn, you shall die." The king went away and left the girl to her task. Now the poor girl did not know how to spin straw into gold. She was very much afraid, and at last she began to cry.

Suddenly the door opened and in stepped a tiny little man who said, "Good evening, Miss Millermaid, why are you weeping?"

"I don't know how to spin this straw into gold," she confessed. Then she told him what the king had said.

"What will you give me if I spin the straw for you?" he asked.

"My handsome necklace!" the girl answered quickly.

The tiny man took the necklace and went to the spinning wheel.
Round and round it went, humming merrily. And right there before
the girl's eyes, the quaint little man spun the straw into gold. His fingers
moved so quickly, and the wheel whirled so fast, that the miller's daughter could not see how the work was done. When the first light of dawn
shone through the window, all the straw had been spun into shining
yellow gold.

The king was surprised and happy to see the gold. But he was greedy. He took the girl into a larger room and told her if she valued her life to spin all the straw in that room into gold before the next morning.

Again the poor girl cried, and again the little man came and said, "What will you give me if I spin this straw for you?"

"I'll give you the ring on my finger," she offered.

The man took the ring. Again the wheel sang and soon the straw was spun. Still the king was not satisfied. He took the miller's daughter into a yet larger room full of straw and said: "If you spin all this straw into gold this night, you shall become my bride."

When the girl was alone, the little man came once more and asked: "What will you give me to spin this straw for you?"

"I have nothing more to give you," replied the girl sadly.

"Promise me that when you are queen you will give me your first child," suggested the little man.

The unhappy girl did not know what to do, but at last she promised. When the king came, the straw was all spun into gold.

Now the king was satisfied. He led the miller's daughter from the room and she became the queen.

She forgot all about the little man and was very happy when her beautiful baby boy was born. Then one day, all of a sudden, the little man appeared.

"Now give me what you promised!" he said.

The queen offered him all her riches if he would allow her to keep her baby, but he refused. Then the queen wept so sorrowfully that the little man felt pity for her.

"If you can guess my name in three days, you may keep him," he said, and went away as suddenly as he had come.

The queen and her ladies thought of all the names they knew. Messengers were sent all over the land to learn of any new names.

When the tiny man came next day the queen guessed Timothy, Benjamin, Jeremiah; on the second day she guessed Bandy-legs and Crook-shanks, but always the man cried: "That is not my name!"

On the third day one of the messengers returned to the queen. He said: "Yesterday as I was climbing a hill I saw a little hut and before it a funny little man danced around a fire singing:

'Merrily the feast I'll make, today I'll brew, tomorrow bake;
Merrily I'll dance and sing, for next day will a stranger bring;
Little deems my little dame, that Rumpelstiltzkin is my name.'"

Soon the little man appeared. "What's my name?" he asked.

"Is it Conrad? Or may it be Harry?" guessed the queen.

"That is not my name!" shouted the strange little man.

"Is it Rumpelstiltzkin?"

At that name he screamed, "Some witch told you! Some witch told you!" and in a rage he stamped his right foot so hard that he sank down through the floor and out of sight. From that time forward, the queer little man was seen no more.

Goldilocks and the Three Bears

ONCE upon a time there were three Bears who lived in a little house in a big forest. There was the great big Father Bear who spoke in a deep voice. There was the middle-sized Mother Bear who spoke in a middle-sized voice, and there was a little tiny Baby Bear who spoke in a high, squeaky voice.

Each had a bowl for his oatmeal;—a great big bowl for the Father Bear, a middle-sized bowl for the Mother Bear, and a tiny bowl for the Baby Bear. Each had a chair to sit in;—a great big chair for the Father Bear, a middle-sized chair for the Mother Bear, and a little tiny chair for the Baby Bear.

One morning when Mother Bear had filled their bowls with oatmeal for breakfast, they found it was too hot to eat, so Father Bear said, "Let us take a walk in the big forest while our oatmeal cools."

There was a little girl called Goldilocks, because her hair was

the color of gold, who wandered far in the big forest to pick flowers. She came to the little house while the Bears were out walking. Goldilocks liked the little house so much that she knocked on the door—knock! knock! knock! Of course no one answered so she walked right in.

Goldilocks was so hungry, when she saw the oatmeal, she said, "Yum! Yum! I'll eat some of that." She tasted the oatmeal in Father Bear's bowl. "It's too hot!" she said. Then she tasted the oatmeal in Mother Bear's bowl. "It's too cold!" she said. Then she tasted the oatmeal in Baby Bear's bowl. "Yummy, it's just right!" she said, and ate it all up.

"Now I'll sit down and rest," said Goldilocks. So she tried Father Bear's big chair. "This is too hard," she said. Then she tried Mother Bear's chair. "This is too soft," she said. Then she tried Baby Bear's chair. "This is just right!" But she sat down so hard that she broke the little chair all to pieces.

Goldilocks was so tired that she went upstairs and got into Father Bear's bed. "This is too hard." Then she tried Mother Bear's bed. "This is too soft." Then she tried Baby Bear's bed. "This is just right!" And soon she was fast asleep.

The Three Bears came back to their little house. "Somebody's been eating my oatmeal," growled Father Bear in his deep voice. "Somebody's been eating my oatmeal," said Mother Bear in her middle-sized voice. "Somebody's been eating my oatmeal and has *eaten it all up!*" cried Baby Bear in his squeaky voice.

Then the Three Bears looked at their chairs. "Somebody's been sitting in my chair," growled Father Bear in his deep voice. "Somebody's been sitting in my chair," said Mother Bear in her middle-sized voice. "Somebody sat in my chair, and *broke it all to pieces!*" cried

Baby Bear in his squeaky voice.

"Growl, growl!" said Father Bear. "I'm going upstairs and find out who's in our house." So Father Bear, and Mother Bear, and Baby Bear, all climbed up the stairs to their bedrooms to find out who was in their house.

"Somebody's been tumbling my bed!" growled Father Bear in his deep voice. "Somebody's been tumbling my bed!" said Mother Bear in her middle-sized voice. "Somebody's been tumbling my bed, and oh, come quick! Here she is!" squealed Baby Bear in his high, squeaky voice.

Goldilocks had been dreaming and when she heard Father Bear's deep growl it sounded like a storm outside and it did not wake her. And Mother Bear's voice sounded like the waterfall in the big forest and it did not wake her. But the high, squeaky voice of Baby Bear woke Goldilocks.

The Three Bears were so surprised when Goldilocks woke that they just stood with their mouths open while Goldilocks scrambled out of bed. She ran to the window and jumped out into the soft pine needles.

The little house was so low that it did not hurt Goldilocks to jump out the window. She ran all the way home while the Three Bears watched from the window. And though Goldilocks often went into the big forest, she never saw the little house again.

Three Little Kittens

THREE little kittens
They lost their mittens,
And they began to cry,

"Oh! mammy dear,
We sadly fear
Our mittens we have lost!"

"What! lost your mittens, you naughty kittens!
Then you shall have no pie!"
Miew, miew, miew, miew,
Miew, miew, miew, miew.

The three little kittens
They found their mittens
And they began to cry,

"Oh! mammy dear,
See here, see here!
Our mittens we have found!"

"What! found your mittens, you little kittens!
Then you shall have some pie!"
Purr, purr, purr, purr,
Purr, purr, purr, purr.

233 ✦✦✦

The three little kittens
Put on their mittens,
And soon ate up their pie;

"Oh! mammy dear,
We greatly fear
Our mittens we have soiled!"

"What! soiled your mittens, you naughty kittens!"
Then they began to sigh,
Miew, miew, miew, miew,
Miew, miew, miew, miew.

The three little kittens
They washed their mittens
And hung them up to dry;

"Oh! mammy dear,
    Look here, look here,
        Our mittens we have washed!"

"What! washed your mittens, you darling kittens!
But I smell a rat close by!"
Rush! hush! miew, miew,
Miew, miew, miew, miew.

The Three Little Pigs

ONCE three little pigs said
good-bye to their mother and
went out to seek their fortunes.

One pig met a man who gave him some straw. The pig built himself a straw house.

The wolf said, "Let me in!"
"Not by the hair of my chinny, chin, chin!"
the pig said.

The wolf said, "I'll huff and I'll puff till I blow your house in!" And that's what he did.

The next pig met a man who gave
him some sticks. This pig built a
house of sticks.

The wolf said, "Let me in!"
"Not by the hair of my chinny, chin, chin!"
the pig said.

The wolf said, "I'll huff and I'll
puff till I blow your house in!"
And that's what he did.

The third pig met a man who gave him some bricks. This pig built a brick house.

This time the wolf huffed and puffed till he was tired but could not blow in the house.

Then the pig met the wolf in an orchard. But he threw an apple to the wolf and escaped.

Another day the pig went to the fair.
He rode on the merry-go-round till
he saw the wolf.

The pig bought a churn, got inside it, rolled down the hill and frightened the wolf away.

The wolf did not give up. He went to the little brick house and climbed on the roof.

Down the chimney he went—into
a pot of hot water! So he never
troubled the pigs again.

ALSO AVAILABLE